*An erotic, fantasy
emotion, and huma
to the frank sexuali, ...
witches, shapechangers, demons, and immortal beings. Turn the
page and let them unveil their dark story in the ambiance of
medieval France.*

An **ongoin**g *series, this is a collection of the first three
volumes—*

Volume 1, The Path

*Melisse dreams of another life, one in which she is no longer the
servant to a noble family, one where she can find her own
destiny and make her life her own.*

*On the eve of the arrival of the Marechal de Barristide, an
eldritch light in the forest calls out to her, giving her the hope of
change to come.*

*The Marechal, a man marked with a vicious scar, is a man of
the law of the realm, charged with investigating a series of
horrible crimes to the south. However, he has his own reasons
for visiting House Perene. Reasons that drive him to search
mercilessly for the truth, no matter the cost.*

*His search and the fate of Melisse intertwine to form a tapestry
of lust, violence, and supernatural implications. All of which
resound within a potent and robust story that draws the reader
in and does not let go.*

Volume 2, The Hunter

The sun rises upon the blood soaked House Perene.

Evil has struck within and without and only the Marechal de Barristide can untangle the threads of fate that wind about him in a web of intrigue and passion.

His way is branded into the very ground before him, but the Marechal must turn his course in order to seek aid from a dreaded soul. Beings from a realm other than earth shall seek his alliance while his quarry, the servant woman, Melisse, has disappeared, leaving only ash and dust behind her. But before taking up her trail once more, the Marechal must submit to another's infernal desires and pay far more than he bargained for.

Here continues The Marechal Chronicles, an erotic tale of desire and merciless destruction as the players assemble themselves to pirouette in an intricate clockwork of unflinching sexuality and supernatural forces.

Volume 3, The Prey

The paths of the Marechal de Barristide and Melisse, runaway servant accused of a grisly murder, narrow to convergence in a seamy quarter of Licharre, a city bordering the Ardoise mountains to the south.

Lust and desire burn all that lies between them as demons rear their ugly heads, twisting their destinies together while powers beyond those of mankind exact their vile desires.

Blood will run before it is over and doom shall fall where it will in this continuing story of supernatural passion and erotic romance.

This edition now includes the prequel story, The Goblin Between Her Thighs.

The Marechal Chronicles:
Volumes I, II and III

(An Erotic Fantasy Tale)

Aimélie Aames

TABLE OF CONTENTS

THE MARECHAL CHRONICLES: VOLUME 1, THE PATH

He twined himself about her, his tongue stretching out to lap at her silky skin.

"I'm telling you, there is something wrong," she said as he continued to wind himself around her, golden, liquid, the fire quickening within him.

"And *I'm* telling you that this is not the moment, darling," he said it smiling, and tried once more to catch her lips with his own.

Their forms flowed back and forth, two shades of gold, as ephemeral as mist and as light as downy plumes.

However, his mounting passion began to fill him and his shape took hold, rippling muscles sliding under bronze skin, his frame becoming heavy, where her own remained like that of smoke, nearly without definition.

"You're not listening to me," she sighed as his insistent mouth, warm and moist, sought out her own. She acquiesced and felt her own body lifting up out of the golden fire now filling her thoughts.

His hands found the mounds of her breasts, swelling, the nipples hardening in the grasp of his fingers. He slipped his head down, the light roughness of his unshaven chin rasping gently across her belly, his eyes on hers before he dipped down further to let his warm breath fall upon her navel.

She felt her legs opening, and the desire he had awakened within her brought her fully into corporeal form. She lifted herself against him, the sensations keeping her spine arched and her body ready and willing for him.

He moved further down and brushed ever so lightly against her mound with its velvet blond hair before coming to rest with his mouth against the inside of her thigh. His tongue slipped out and traced its way along first one side, then the other.

She moaned, trying to master herself, to hold herself still and not be the instrument of his will. But as his breathing deepened and his tongue made its way to the swell of her leg, she felt heat between her legs, the delicious, moist ache that he had awakened in her.

She knew he was playing her as well as any song, becoming his melody as he composed note after note, writing each with the touch of his tongue and hands.

She forced herself down, her spine protesting, and turned herself around while slipping lower, down past him, only to come back up with her breasts pushing firmly against his back.

He laughed and then turned himself over as well, their positions reversed, as she slipped lower, working her way down his legs.

His penis stood rigid and proud. She could see the strong beat of his heart in its tumescence as she bent over the soft skin of his scrotum. She took it ever so gently between her lips, sucking it inward and then pulling back. Releasing him, she could see his testicles turning, lifting back up to their position, readying themselves. She came at him again with her mouth wide and took one, then the other, into her mouth, rolling them with her tongue and delighting in the movement that this engendered.

Despite himself, his hips began to rock forward, the rhythm slow but sure. Once released from her mouth, his sack lifted up once again, this time with a delightful sensation of cool air where the wet of her mouth had been.

She dipped her head down once more and took his tip between her lips, slipping her tongue across its surface until she found the hole, slick with his mounting desire. She felt him shift under her, knowing that it was probably too much for him to bear, before she fell down and took all of him into her mouth.

The heat of her breath and the fire of her passion caressed him just as firmly as her tongue as it slipped up and down his shaft. The rhythm increased and he could feel himself beginning to tighten, the muscles of his thighs and those of his anus seizing ever tighter. She felt it, too, and wanting the the moment to endure, she ceased her ministrations.

She moved up his body, careful not to touch his member, preferring that the furnace she had ignited within him calm itself.

She licked his nipple and took it between her teeth, pulling it back, daring him to wince because of her bite.

Then it was his turn to come to her and his mouth found her own, his lips plump, her own full, and together they moved in rhythm, until she could stand it no more and slipped his sex inside her.

Her velvet heat enveloped him and he gasped at the suddenness of it. She sank down again and again, each time with more force, each time pushing herself hard against him while grinding her pubis before lifting up to come down once again.

Their hips moved in counterpoint to one another, a staccato clash finding its own rhythm, their breaths shortening and deepening. He felt the tightening once more deep in his abdomen, while she felt herself opening and opening, the desire to take him deeper inside herself driving away all thought.

She felt it then, the tension that had been building inside lifting up and up before it reached its peak, almost as if all her passion had washed away in that tiny instant, balanced upon a pinnacle, all held in equilibrium before the thundering avalanche took her, her muscles fluttering deep inside with the electric sting of her clitoris, deliciously painful, pulling itself back.

He felt her breath catch, the movement of her hips paused for just a moment, and then she groaned deeply, almost guttural in tone, as she flung herself tighter against him. Her legs wrapped around him in desperation, the undulation of her orgasm pulling him onward in the riptide of her pleasure.

He felt himself expand, all of him rock hard and rigid in urgency, his thoughts shrinking down to the pinpoint of the moment, and then the exquisite release came upon him, his body wracked with violent, pumping spasms.

She felt his climax inside her own, her inner thighs fluttering in response, and the heat of him flowed outward, his cock filling her and filling her. His movements became animalistic in nature, instinct and pleasure intermingling in the embrace of her legs. It called forth an echo of response and she felt herself tighten once more before falling down the other side, deep muscles thrumming in heat and rhythm and spent passion.

They lay together, warmth and light encircling them. The bodies of a man and a woman fell into gold, into copper, as what was once solid and human dissolved.

They returned to their incorporeal states, golden fire twining around each other, bathed in blinding light that was both searing heat and numbing ice.

"So, you say that something is wrong, my darling?" he asked.

"Can you not feel it? The fire feels tainted in some way, as if some of it has gone out of our realm," she replied, hesitant.

He waited a moment, searching about him, tasting the flavors of their shared magic.

"Yes, there is something. And as to that, I can only pose a question. Where is your brother?"

The color of her fire dimmed then, as if she had doubts or was ashamed of something.

"I don't know. None of us do."

His voice grew hard then, his flame taking on deep russet tones.

"That there is a risk of corruption seems clear. It shall be sought out and eliminated," he replied. "Woe to your kin if he is at the heart of this, hiding as he does outside our realm with his little friend. It will avail him naught."

Her colors fell cold, tinged with blue. Her voice small, she asked, "What shall we do?"

"*We* shall do nothing. *I*, on the other hand, am calling forth the Evangeline."

To this she had no response except to shudder and turn away.

She leaned close to the rippled glass window pane. There, at the forest's edge, she saw it again, a light that moved back and forth in broad, beckoning motions. Melisse could not imagine how a person might manage to swing a lantern so slowly and so widely. Instead, she watched it, a glowing pendulum of warm inviting light, golden hued like that of a beeswax candle. Except that the distance was too far to make out a candle. Even a lantern of rude oil would be drowned in the unfurling darkness of sunset.

She watched it, fascinated by its glow and the way it seemed to be meant just for her. A light meant to lead her away. A light meant for better things.

Her breath misted against the glass and Melisse shook herself. Her mother would have told her to remember her place, her duty as chambermaid. She turned away from the window and rushed to the fireplace.

Melisse pumped furiously on the bellows, desperate to see the embers in the fireplace whiten in intensity. The two cauldrons poised upon the hearthstones were still barely steaming, little more than tepid in the chill air of the demoiselle Helene's bedchamber.

A light voice hummed a gentle melody in the next room, a sound that mingled well with the splashing of bathwater.

"Melisse! I must have more hot water, girl. The bath cools and I fear catching cold!"

"I'm hurrying, M'lady," Melisse called back, still working the bellows as hard as she could. A bead of sweat ran down her forehead, slipping down to sting her eyes as she pumped away.

The demoiselle was in an adjoining room, a great claw footed bath of hammered copper dominating the space. Her father had ordered the thing in a city to the north and had it brought here at great expense after his daughter had heard of the new mode of bathing and how people might bathe more often than at the two key moments of their lives, at birth and at death.

Melisse had to admit that it seemed sensible to her, although washing down with cold well water while standing upon her own two feet did not seem less efficient.

However, it had always been Helene's way. If some means of luxury was within reach, she would whine and mope about the manor until her father took notice. He then never failed to meet, if not exceed, his children's wishes.

Helene was a beautiful young woman, with thick blond hair prone to escaping her coiffure and tumbling down in a way that was calculated to entice the regard of others. Her pale skin and hourglass form simply completed the effect.

Melisse's own hair was black and drawn back severely in a haphazard bun, all the better to keep it out of her way as she worked. Her own skin was just as pale as that of Helene, her house maiden's life sparing her from the sun, but her figure was heavier and more thickly boned. Her's was a servant's body.

"Never mind the hot water, Melisse", Helene called out. "Just come and help me scrub my back. I can't reach and I want to be sparkling clean to greet my father's guest this evening."

Melisse sighed. She knew Helene enjoyed her games, and amusing herself at Melisse's expense was one of her favorites.

Steeling herself, Melisse left her iron pots at the hearth. As she passed the window with its blurred glass panes, she saw the light in the darkness once more. It seemed as familiar as a friend to her, bobbing with a warm glow deep in the forest. She would have liked to look more closely, to puzzle out its meaning, to tease away some purpose apart from her days in the manor. Instead, she walked into the next room.

Helene was in her bathing chemise. It was woven from sheer linen and while meant for propriety, in water the fine cloth turned instantly transparent.

The demoiselle was reclined, with only her head and neck above the waterline, a thin trace of soap floating on the edges of the water. Hearing Melisse, Helene tilted her head back to rest against the bathtub, at once sighing and lifting her chest into view.

Melisse turned her gaze away, but not before seeing light pink nipples studding the fabric of Helene's bathing shirt. Seeing the scrub brush leaning against the tub, she seized it.

"M'lady, if you'd like me to scrub your back, you'll need to lean forward," Melisse said as she went to her knees. Her voice was nearly a whisper, her tone timid.

Helene opened her eyes then, searching for those of Melisse, except that Melisse's gaze was turned down, as if she found the stone floor more interesting ... or less frightening.

"You know, Melisse, if we put your hair up correctly and got you out of that potato sack you're wearing, I think you'd be surprised at how pretty you could be."

Despite herself, Melisse looked up and into Helene's eyes, finding a smile there. The green color held her and she let Helene take her hand with the brush in it and guide her closer to the water.

Helene held the brush to her belly, her breasts lifted fully into view, and said, "Just there, my dear Melisse. Scrub there, but do it gently."

Melisse began scrubbing and turned her head away. Helene sighed and began humming the melody once more.

Her grip was too light in her efforts to be gentle and the handle of the brush turned in her hand. Helene hissed and seized Melisse's arm.

"Pay attention, dullard! You can't do it right while staring at the wall."

Helene clamped her hand over Melisse's and directed the brush back to her stomach, saying, "I'm going to show you, just this once, how one should brush clean the delicate skin of a noblewoman."

Her hand still holding Melisse's and the brush together, Helene began making circles against her belly and with each she descended lower and lower until the brush began to touch her thighs.

She said, "Oops...let's change the technique, shall we, dear?" And began moving it up and down in long straight movements that soon dropped down fully between her legs.

She opened her mouth just a little and Melisse could see how red her lips had become. The tip of Helene's tongue slipped out to moisten them and Melisse saw that its color was exactly the same as her nipples, clearly visible through the taut linen shirt.

Deeper down the brush went until Helene began to slide down into the water with it, her eyes closed and making little mewling sounds, reminding Melisse of a hungry kitten.

"Now...just don't...stop," Helene gasped as she let go of Melisse's hand.

Melisse continued the long stroking motion of the brush and did her best to unfocus her eyes, looking for some means of distancing herself from her mistress in the bath.

The water had already turned quite cool and sloshed about as Helene moved in time against the brush in Melisse's grasp.

"Please, m'Lady, I'll go get the water now. I'm sure it's quite hot," she said, dropping the brush and pulling back her hand as if the cool water had just scalded her.

Helene's eyes flew open and Melisse saw there a raw flash of emotion, one that she knew little of, yet recognized all the same. Even the lowest dog in the kennels would recognize it and understand it in its most basic sense. Burning hatred flashed like an ember bursting in the hearth before dimming as quickly as it came. Helene was of noble blood and had learned early how to cover one's thoughts as quickly as need be.

"Oh, my dear," she said, mastering herself and smiling. "Look at the color burning in your cheeks. Have I done something to spark such heat?"

She languidly took up the floating brush and began the same long strokes down her abdomen with it.

"Yes, m'lLady…I mean, no," Melisse stammered, backing away.

Helene held her eye while the strokes of the brush took on a stronger rhythm. The vicious glint was back in her eyes as she said, "Or, is it not me then, dear Melisse? Perhaps your color is from thinking of my brother while helping me to bathe? You were imagining him here, his handle in your hands as you stroke it up and down, deeper and quicker…."

Helene's breath had changed. It came in short, shallow bursts. She dropped the brush then plunged her hand in the water between her raised thighs, her knees rocking in time with her arm.

Her unflinching gaze held Melisse as the words left her and light whimpering sounds slipped between her lips. She didn't blink as she rubbed herself steadily and Melisse could not break away.

Her lips were suffused in rich red and Melisse watched as Helene clenched her jaw. She drew her lips back in what might have passed for a smile in any other occasion, but only reminded Melisse of a mad dog. The skin of her cheeks was pulled tight, held in her grimace, and then her hips lifted up, nearly out of the water, holding still an instant before falling down slowly in small stuttering movements.

Helene let her breath out in one long sigh, slipping down into the water once more.

"Don't just stand there, you fool. Fetch my hot water."

Melisse did not wait to be told a second time.

The Marechal de Barristide watched the nobleman pace back and forth before the row of windows that ran the length of the room. His steps were measured and stiff. When he turned around to come back in the Marechal's direction, he turned on his heel with all the precision of a military man who had not forgotten his days upon the battle field.

He stopped pacing once before a window with a view onto what must be a rose garden, although to the Marechal's eyes it seemed a dying thing. The flowers had long since fallen with the coming of the cool nights of autumn.

"My apologies, Marechal. The attention to detail of our house servants is not what it once was. I've been too lax. If my father had ever had to wait on a carafe of wine, why the entire lot of them would have been turned out to the horse yard and whipped until he was sure they were, each and every one, wide awake and attentive to their duties."

Lord Perene turned on his heel once more, his hands clasped behind him and his hooked nose seeming to cut the air before him as he paced.

The Marechal watched him a moment longer, then said, "Even if the road was long, Lord Perene, my throat has been drier than this. I'll not die of thirst, I assure you. At least, not today."

"That is very understanding of you," said the nobleman as a young man bustled into the library carrying a platter of silver cups and a pitcher.

Lord Perene walked briskly over to him, not saying a word as the servant placed the wine service on a small table in the corner.

Before the young man could take up the carafe, Lord Perene struck him with his closed fist, a short, chopping blow that put the young man instantly to his knees. His look was one of surprise before his eyes rolled up and he crumpled the rest of the way to the floor.

The muscles in the Marechal's jaw bunched tightly, and the scar that snaked like a lightning strike along his cheek and down his neck whitened. The odor of urine filled the air.

"Would you look at that," said the gray haired nobleman, an almost frantic smile on his face. "The idiot pissed himself."

Melisse tried to make herself small in a corner of the steamy kitchen. The noise of pots and pans clanging and banging, the cooks shouting to one another as the kitchen boys hauled in crates of vegetables, all of it, the confusion and the tumult was a comfort to her. Familiar, happy sounds. Sounds she had known all her life.

"Melisse! What are ya doin' there, girl? M'lady will be ripe to pitch a fit if yer not there to dress 'er."

Mathilde's cheeks were bright red and her nose held a drop of sweat just at the end. No matter how she turned her head about, the drop just dangled there, defiant. Her old smock was dusted with flour and Melisse could see some of it in her hair, mingling with the gray and giving her ten years more than poor Mathilde deserved.

"She sent me away, Mathilde. She said I was boring her, "Melisse replied. Out of habit, she raised her voice to be heard over the sounds of the kitchen. It was another reason that she loved being there so. She could come close to shouting when the kitchen was full of noisy cooking men and women. Nowhere else did she feel at liberty enough to dare speaking in just over a whisper. Her mother had taught her well.

"Sent away or no, she'll be screamin' bloody murder soon enough. And us, shorthanded already."

A few minutes earlier, the gardener and the stableman had come in to the kitchen, dragging young Oscar between them. He was slumped like all the air had gone out of him and Melisse had watched, frightened, as they slapped him awake.

He came around eventually, his head still lolling loosely before he caught Melisse looking at him. He gave her a lopsided grin. She had seen the blood at the corner of his mouth and the tooth Lord Perene had broken. Someone laughed and said he had been lucky not to have choked on it.

Mathilde sized up what needed to be done as the old veteran of the household that she was. "Ruthie! Get over here and never mind those lettuces."

Ruthie, knowing Mathilde was not one for indecision, dropped the wilted leaves she had been stripping away and took up the great wooden spoon at Mathilde's place.

"Mind the stew, Ruthie. It's got nothing but simmering to do now, but it'll need stirring or it'll stick and burn, turning the whole unfit for m'Lord and his guest."

She undid her apron, dusting herself off as well as she could. "Melisse, I'll go upstairs and get the lady dressed. She'll keep her hands to herself if it's me standing before her, I'll wager."

Melisse supposed she was right. Mathilde's youth was long past and there was little risk that her dowdy figure would interest Helene.

But at Mathilde's next words, her heart sank.

"We're stretched too thin so yer'll be goin' to wait on m'Lord and the Marechal. Keep yer eyes open and yer mouth shut. Do as yer told and do it quick and all should go well enough. Lord Perene always appreciated yer mother and I don't see as how he could hit the daughter. Leastways, not in front of a guest, I mean."

The Marechal swirled the wine in his cup, searching for a little more body in its depths. Sadly, he doubted he would find anything more, no matter how much air it was shown. The Lord Perene was known to be a rich man, but his wine was as insipid as his demeanor.

They had removed themselves to the library as servants rushed in to clean the mess in the reception hall. The Marechal himself had proposed it, intrigued after having heard of Lord Perene's library and its selection of rare and specialized oeuvres.

A fire had been quickly laid in the library's hearth and the servants busied themselves with the less than customary idea of serving dinner in the manor's library.

The reason for the Marechal's coming was seated before him, at a great table of oak in the center of the room. Books bound in various leathers and reams of parchment had been swept away while Lord Perene's son looked about him vacantly, the corners of his mouth stained red. The color was high in his cheeks and his eyes turned lazily in their orbits.

"As I was saying, Marechal. It is with no small thanks that we welcome you here to our house," said Lord Perene. His back was to the Marechal as he appeared to examine the shelves of books before him.

"Now that my son is of age, entering his name into the official registers as my heir is of great importance to me. All that I have shall pass to him, with no means of disputing his claim once we have your seal upon the appropriate documents and they are filed at the prefecture in Barristide."

The Marechal replied, "Rest assured, Lord Perene, the proprietorship of the Perene family line shall be in good hands. But, setting aside these official matters, I confess that my interest in coming here is in no small part one of curiosity concerning the reputation of your library and the works collected here.

"I have heard rumors that you've had the good fortune of finding something relating to Urrune and its most famous denizen."

The nobleman scowled and said, "Which is why we have been honored by your presence rather than one of your undersecretaries. I see. And to think that it is not quite the importance of our family that has brought you here after all, but merely a matter of...books."

The Marechal stood up then, placed his wine upon the table, and bent low at the waist in a sweeping bow. His height was great for a man of the region, making his effort all the more dramatic.

"It was not my intention to offend you, Lord Perene. Neither you, nor your house. As it happens, there have been a series of grisly murders to the south of here and the local magistrates have been perfectly ineffectual in rooting out the villain behind them. They had sent word for my aid some weeks ago, so it seemed reason enough to pass by here in order to give you my personal attention before continuing southward.

"And yes, I have a weakness for books. Particularly, historical works of the region."

As if he had heard only one word of the Marechal's explanation, the bleary-eyed lord's son said, "Murders? Just how grisly are they?"

The Marechal's scar jumped under the bunching muscles of his jaw.

"Apparently, the victims have been found fully clothed, yet each had been expertly skinned."

Lord Perene turned around then, his gaze falling upon his son, and said, "Olivier, I'll thank you not to speak until spoken to. You've been drinking. Anything worthwhile you might have had to say has been washed down your gullet."

A door to the library quietly opened and closed in a remote corner and the Marechal saw a young, mousy woman in servant's attire standing there. Her hair was tied back in a severe, no nonsense bun and she kept her eyes cast downwards. He noted that if there was one remarkable thing about her, it was her perfect ordinariness, a resolute manner of appearing unnoticed and invisible.

But the lord's son noticed, saying, "Melisse. How wonderful that you're here. Please come sit on my lap and distract me from all this boring talk of books and papers."

The Marechal saw her face redden, and it seemed to him that if she could have made herself even smaller, she would have. She did not reply to the lord's son, only curtseying slightly before walking dutifully over to take up the wine pitcher. She served the Marechal first and he smelled apples and lilac at her passage.

As she filled Lord Perene's cup, he said, "There's a good girl. I was always pleased with your mother's service, Melisse. It's a shame that a fever should have taken her."

Melisse only mumbled, "Yes, m'lord", before moving on to Olivier.

His own cup was still on the table and he made no move to offer it to Melisse. She leaned past him for it and he encircled her narrow waist in his arms.

Her face flaming red, she said, "M'lord, please!"

But the drunken young man only laughed, saying, "Oh, Melisse, I've seen how you look at me from the corner of your eyes when you think no one notices. I've seen that and more. You might as well have written it in a formal invitation, dear girl."

The Marechal set his cup once more upon the table, and none too lightly, before bringing his own gaze to bear on that of the young man. He said nothing, but he was a man of considerable physical stature and the threat written in his eyes was clear.

Olivier swallowed and let go his grasp upon Melisse. Shaking, she filled his cup and set it down quickly before stepping back to her place by the small door through which she had come.

The thought that she would like to turn and flee through that small door in the corner was clear to the Marechal. That she held to her duty and stayed instead had more courage to it than anything he had yet seen in the house of Perene.

Lord Perene looked from the Marechal to his son and back again, a look of disgust spreading across his visage. He turned then, back to the shelves of books and reached up to take one down, its binding cracked under the weight of centuries.

"So, books of history. Even more specifically, a history of Urrune and who else, if not the famed Alchemist of Urrune."

The Marechal's eyes opened wider and he strode over to the nobleman's side.

"So it is true. You have Bellamere's recounting of the legend of the Alchemist," breathed the Marechal. His focus became even more intense as he took in the brittle pages being turned in the hands of Lord Perene.

Despite his displeasure of a moment earlier, Lord Perene smiled with pride.

"What's more is that the text even includes a name for one of the principles in the legend. It cites the apprentice as being a certain Etienne St. Lucq, and that he and the Alchemist were inseparable from all accounts. I believe it is the only mention of anyone's name in all known accounts, in fact.

"However, Bellamere was certainly quite mad, I'm afraid. But yes, the tome is his. It is surprisingly lucid when one considers what is described here. The Alchemist's alliance with witches and the fruitless search for life unending. All of it coming to the devastating end of the Alchemist and this St. Lucq personage in a violent explosion that is even today thought to be the reason that his tower lies there, in ruin."

Narrowing his eyes, Lord Perene asked, "Have you seen it? Urrune is not that far from Barristide, as I recall."

"Yes," replied the Marechal, "I've had occasion to pass through the region. The tower is there in a tumbled heap and not a blade of green grass grows within half a league of it.

"The local folk believe it a cursed place, all the life sucked dry and apt to stay that way for centuries more, they say."

Lord Perene closed the book, a quizzical look on his face.

"Even after all this time, nothing grows there?" he asked. "Why it seems quite impossible...these events date to three centuries in the past."

The Marechal nodded. "Nevertheless. Be it three hundred years or six weeks ago, nothing lives in the environs. Apparently, the calamity that destroyed the Alchemist and his tower continues on in some fashion."

Lord Perene motioned for more wine while he considered the Marechal's words.

"Most remarkable," he murmured as Melisse hurried over to fill his cup.

The Marechal saw that despite her timid mien, she was confident and self-assured in her service. She went to the nobleman with quick, light steps and poured his wine without spilling a drop.

As she went to resume her place in the corner of the library, Olivier seized her by her ample hips. Unbalanced, she lost her grip on the silver wine pitcher and upended most of its contents down the young man's front.

He snarled and caught one of her breasts in his hand as if it were a fruit and wrenched it viciously. Melisse screamed and in a flash, she struck his face open handed with a cracking sound that echoed in the room.

The Marechal held his own cup, his knuckles whitening, as Lord Perene shouted with a voice that had become almost girlish in tone.

"Melisse! Get out, get out now…get out of this house. And you, Olivier, my *heir*," the word twisted in his mouth, "you are a drunken fool to behave like this before an honored guest. You seek courage in a wine cup, except that this time you have fallen down among the dregs…my *son*."

The small servants' door in the corner slammed shut as a white-faced Melisse fled.

An instant later, the library's principal door opened and in walked a young woman as graceful and elegant as the young man was slovenly and dull-witted.

"Ah," breathed Lord Perene, "A breath of fresh air to sweeten a moment turned sour. Marechal, my daughter, Helene."

She was reed thin with what was surely luxurious blond hair that had been carefully done up in an elaborate coiffure. Her pale skin was a perfect counterpoint to her full, red lips, only to finish with green eyes worthy of the most aloof feline.

Seeing her wine-soaked brother sprawled loosely in his chair and her father, his severe expression only now softening as she took in the room, she curtseyed deeply before the Marechal.

She smiled, revealing small perfect teeth that reminded the Marechal of a child's mouth, except that the smile of this young woman never reached her eyes.

"Marechal, I am pleased to make your acquaintance. It would seem that my brother is enough at ease in your presence to jest...in his way. So it would seem that I shall find my own ease just as quickly, although my humor is, perhaps, more subtle than his."

The Marechal bowed low as before, and Helene took in his large square shoulders that hinted at well-muscled arms hidden within his loose chemise.

"M'lady Perene," he said as he straightened.

"'Demoiselle', Marechal. At least, that is, until my father finds a suitor for me worthy of association with House Perene." Her brother snorted at this, as though he found her words preposterous.

Helene ignored him, continuing smoothly, "But, please, Marechal, do me the honor of my first name," she replied, her smile growing wider.

"As you wish...Helene."

She paused, waiting for the Marechal to answer in kind. At his silence, she turned lightly away, toward her father.

"Oh Father, please smile for me. Is it not for a marvelous occasion, the naming of my brother as heir, that we are here? Surely this is cause enough for good humor and light-hearted talk."

Lord Perene smiled then. It faded quickly, though, as he said, "Yes, the naming of an heir...a cruel, foolish boy. Would that you had born differently, Helene. That would be reason for celebration."

The Marechal saw her smile widen ever more and despite her beauty, he could not help but be reminded of a serpent. A grinning animal remorselessly opening wide its maw, preparing to swallow down its prey.

The clamor of the kitchen was even worse than before and Melisse quickly slipped through the bustling cooks to find her small corner not far from the wood fired stoves.

Mathilde was back at her stew pot and saw the young woman pass by as quietly as a ghost. When she turned to look at her more closely, she saw that there was more to her that was ghostlike, as white as her face had become.

"Melisse! There you are again, come back and back same's a stubborn cough. But what's got the color wiped clean out of you, girl?"

Melisse swallowed and said, "Lord Perene sent me away, Mathilde."

"Aye, that's plain to see. But why are you so pale?" the older woman replied.

"I slapped m'lord Olivier and then his father told me to get out of his sight and out of his home. Oh, what am I going to do, Mathilde?"

The dam broke and Melisse's tears flowed freely. Mathilde shrieked, "Ruthie!". She dropped her wooden spoon and came over to dab at Melisse's tears with the hem of her apron.

"There, there…t'will be alright, Melisse. His lord didn't mean it, not really. He knows his boy is too fond of the red and if you hit him, it was surely deserved.

"The trick will be just to keep you out of sight for a a day or two and afore long, Lord Perene will come 'round, I know it."

The concern in Mathilde's eyes was as genuine as Melisse's fear, and she held onto the cook's words as tightly as she could.

"Tell me, Mathilde…where shall I go?"

"To start, Melisse, take a turn at dumping the slops bucket. The slops boy ran off a week ago and we've all had a hand at carrying the thing 'round back. You take a turn and then you take your time and instead of coming back here when yer done, go find a warm corner in the stables. I'll send word that yer coming and they'll take care that yer well and safe, dear."

And then, being the cook that she was and wanting to help in the way that she understood, Mathilde brought her two golden brown bread rolls, still steaming from the oven, their interiors layered with apple purée and autumn spices.

Melisse ate them, nearly burning her tongue before Mathilde gave her a cool glass of milk, as if she were a child and not a woman of twenty one years. But Mathilde knew her business and Melisse could not help but smile back at the worried cook as the rolls and milk had their desired effect, comforting her in a way that no words ever could.

Melisse slipped through the kitchen's back door, all the warmth, noise, and delicious smells at her back. The manor's grounds were quiet before her, the close clipped lawn strewn with dew and the glow of the manor's interior did not travel far into the surrounding darkness.

She held the heavy bucket, doing her best to keep the foul thing, filled with rotten vegetables and other noxious things, away from her skirt as she made her way to the back of the manor and the pig enclosure there.

The fallen night was calm with only a small breeze to rattle the few dried leaves stubbornly holding to their branches. She tried to keep her eyes on the pathway around the manor when, from the corner of her eye, she saw it.

At first, it seemed a little thing, easily dismissed, but then it burgeoned as it had earlier, the warm glow of its golden light swinging lazily in the air. It seemed to be just at the edge of the lawn and Melisse strained to see who might be there.

"Hello?" she said in nearly a whisper.

The light seemed to pause in its gentle arc, then resumed its swaying movement. Melisse could not have said why, but she was suddenly quite sure that it was calling her name. Except that her name had become golden hued, in rich beeswax candle colors, and there was no sound in it.

She was halfway to the edge of the manor's lawn when she realized she no longer carried the slops bucket. She turned to look back, seeing the manor and its many windows, the life of the privileged and those who served them written in its facade. Melisse found that it was not so difficult to turn her back upon it and them as the light before her beckoned once more.

At first, it seemed as though the trees parted as she passed. Their branches turned away from her and the underbrush, in its turn, gave way before her.

In fact, it was a path she followed under the moon's light. It was lined in soft, green moss and the going was not difficult.

The bobbing light danced at a distance from her, and she imagined that it was pleased in the way its movements had become more exaggerated and clear in its intent that Melisse should follow.

The moon came and went as she slipped calmly forward, following the bobbing light. At times, certain trees were stubborn before the inevitability that was autumn and the cold months to follow. In those pockets of shadow under clinging leaves, with the moon tucked away and the golden light fallen from her sight, Melisse knew doubt and questioned her reasons for doing something so removed from her character.

But as she walked farther under the familiar moon with the charm of the beeswax candle glow before her, she felt once more at ease and sure that if ever she would change the story that was hers, it was now.

In time, however, it began to feel like hours had passed as her feet began to ache and ever forward the light beckoned her. She chanced to look behind her once, only to to see that the gentle track she was following was not there. Behind her, there was only a rude slope of rocky terrain crisscrossed by menacing, thorny briars. Except that she had no recollection of having descended any hill, thorny or otherwise.

The glow beckoned to her and showed her the way forward upon soft moss and moist leaves that did not crackle beneath her feet.

As she rounded a bend in the path, there before her was a fire burning upon the ground and just beyond, seated upon the ground, a young man.

His smile was full and kind, and any alarm she felt was smoothed over by his somehow familiar visage. The fire burned bright and she could not see all of him, but that his shoulders and chest were bare was plain.

"Hello," she said, as quietly as ever.

The young man made no sign that he had heard her. He only continued to smile and patted the ground beside him.

Melisse stepped around the fire, her own smile answering his, and then came to a sudden stop. Beyond the fire's glare, she could see that he was not wearing a stitch of clothing and what was more, that he had a full erection sprouting from his lap.

"Oh! I'm sorry," she said, turning about upon her heel, feeling the heat rising in her face.

"For what?" he asked. His voice was low and gentle, absurdly calm despite the obvious.

"Is it not a lovely night, a cool autumn breeze wafting around us as we warm our tired bodies before the fire? I am not sorry, nor should you be."

She heard music in his voice, as if he were only half a breath away from singing and she knew his song would be of a heart of warmth in the forest, of two bodies holding the cold world and its harsh truths at bay, if only for a short time, if only for a few stolen moments under the watchful moon.

"Please, do not fear. Come sit beside me and we shall share the warmth." He said it as if he spoke of sharing a cup of wine, even if she felt understanding of the difference was somehow blurred and lacking the edges of meaning that most people employ.

She turned back to him slowly, willing her eyes upon his face, and stepped gingerly toward him. Her movements were hesitant and her body tense, ready to spring away like a wild deer or some other creature of the forest. She traced the lines of his collarbone with her eyes as she found her place just beside him, a finger's breadth of distance between them.

He leaned forward, with his knees up, to gaze into the depths of the fire burning before them. She felt herself drawn to him in the same way that any fire draws the eyes of those near it. She followed the curve of the nape of his neck, seeing the tiny curls at the base of his skull, the way that they turned in all directions, wild, yet charming in the way of boys and men, uninterested in mundane things like well combed hair, saving instead their concentration for more important things like open fires or women alone in the forest.

His shoulders were broad, the bones framing what he would be one day, a robust and well muscled man. Even if he must have been the same age as her, Melisse could see that he had not yet come into his own. The heavy, hard flesh of manhood was just beginning to find its place upon him.

His back curved delicately and she could make out the tiny ridges of the bones of his spine. She couldn't help but wonder what it would be like to lay her hand there, placing her fingers in between the depressions, to feel where his vulnerabilities lie, if he would allow it.

She shivered then, surprised with the turnings her thoughts had taken.

Once more, he smiled a broad, inviting smile. "Now I *am* sorry, in truth. You are cold and I have done nothing to warm you."

With a slight nudge, he closed the distance between them, laying his hand upon her thigh. The heat of him was strong and Melisse shivered again under his touch.

He laughed then and the music in his voice was plain. He leaned in close to her, placing himself fully against her, and despite her trembling at his touch, Melisse did not move away.

His eyes were amber as he looked at her and she felt them pull her in. In that moment, she thought that she might still resist, that there might still be a chance of escaping him. Then she sighed, falling into his depths, letting herself drown in the waters of his golden hued gaze.

His lips were like velour and tasted of honey. His tongue slipped between her teeth and she laughed in surprise. She had not known what a smile could feel like as she felt one form against her lips for the first time, writing itself in answer as they kissed in the warmth of the fire. She could have believed that their teeth struck sparks, brushing together briefly, their smiles intermingling.

He moved his hands about her body, touching her, gently calming her at each point that she stiffened with the shock of his hands touching everywhere and nowhere anyone ever had but her.

He undid laces and buttons with ease, casting aside the conventions of propriety as easily as the wind casts fallen leaves whither it will. The heat of him was full upon her skin as her clothing fell away, as she let herself fall down on the soft ground.

Hungrily, he licked at the base of her throat before coming back to suckle at her ears, his breath tickling her while it seemed to pull at threads inside her, threads that reached down her body, to knot together between her legs.

He took each of her nipples, one after the other, into his mouth, gently. Pulling at them, teasing, before nipping lightly with his teeth. She gasped as he did it, then leaned toward him, her body asking that he do it again.

He lowered himself upon her and she could feel his heavy erection, stiff with warmth, press across her flat stomach. He brought himself level once more and held her face in his gaze, and she felt the desire flowing from him in waves, as heat from flames, and she delighted in his touch, in the intensity of his gaze upon her. It was another first for her. She felt desirable, the focus of all his intentions, that she could be beautiful, even if only for a little while, as he placed her and only her at the center of all his thoughts.

She rocked against him, moaning, at once afraid and hopeful at what would happen. She had been told that it would hurt, except that the ache she felt between her legs, the wetness that was both hot in its urgency and cool as the night air caressed her fine hairs there, the ache demanded only that he answer in the best way of any man.

And so he did. He pulled back from her, lowering his pelvis between her thighs, and she welcomed his movements, almost ashamed at how easily she ceded, but so desperate that it should happen.

He pushed himself forward and she felt his penis touch her there, just at the lips' edges, holding himself still as she quietly cried out. She moved against him, tilting her hips up and down, his tip just within the folds of her lips, the sensation delicious in its thick, wet rhythm. She felt her clitoris hardening ever more, and was reminded of the sting of salt and lemon upon her tongue..

He held himself, unmoving, controlling his desire until his own body shook, the strain showing in his shoulders and in the way that his smile slowly disappeared, to be replaced by a concentration that only heightened Melisse's excitement. Her thoughts came in, erratic, small bursts—that it was about to happen, that it had not happened, that she wanted it more than anything, and that she was afraid.

He seemed to know her mind and so held himself ever still, until she cared nothing more for the rumors she had heard, until her fear melted in the heat of the fire they had ignited.

Her breaths had become short, quick things, and finally, she panted just one syllable. "Please," in answer to the question he had not asked.

Released from his self-restraint, he shuddered, his muscles rippling down the length of his body, and then pushed himself forward, into the cleft that she had opened for him. She welcomed him with a gasp of pleasure.

They rocked together, his hips rolling like breakers upon her shore, the waves rose and clashed, each one lifting the other higher. Melisse had expected pain and embarrassment but felt only release and pleasure as she cradled his cock inside her, lifting against him and with him, their rhythm feeding upon itself.

And as sweat broke out upon both their bodies, Melisse felt him growing ever larger inside her, bigger and bigger, as her legs strained and parted ever farther. Heavy sounds began deep in his chest, throaty and profound, until she realized that he was growling with each thrust of his hips. She opened her eyes to a world aflame, the fire beside them having burned to within an inch of her. Melisse was forced to squint her eyes as golden color suffused her vision, as she saw that the amber of his eyes reflected the fire with a heat all its own.

She turned her face away from him and, in doing so, saw that the fire so comforting earlier had burned very close to them then,, but more than this, and worse than this, she saw that it burned upon nothing. There were no coals at its heart, no logs nor branches set to spend themselves in its hunger. It was simply a golden fire upon the ground, burning itself out upon nothing.

She realized then that it was not the fire reflected in his eyes. She had been mistaken. The fire itself was the reflection of him and all that animated him.

His lips peeled back from his bared teeth in a snarl, his lovely smile twisting into something unrecognizable. She felt his size, become nearly impossible for her to contain, as bestial sounds erupted into the night air.

Despite herself, she was unable to break the rhythm, thrusting against him, even while believing that she was tearing apart inside, and helpless to do anything but invite him onward. The drum of their act pounded out its primitive rhythm.

Tears rolled from the corners of her eyes and suddenly, with three quick, stabbing thrusts, he erupted inside her. She felt herself ripping as burning fire filled her up from inside, a vast, black cauldron of molten color flowing out from him, burning her alive.

She smelled smoke as he drove himself deep inside her once more, a howl ripping from his throat that sounded of all the fall bonfires she had ever known, falling down at festival's end in a heap of white, glowing ash and embers.

Her legs and arms did not obey her as he slowly lifted himself off her chest while still inside her. His hair was smoking and she could see wisps of smoke seeping from eyes that had become filled with inhuman amber, the pupils effaced. She could feel him pumping rhythmically into her despite her sense of having been broken inside, left in ruin.

He smiled down at her and in a gravelly voice not at all like the earlier young man, he said, "You've got what you came for, foolish woman. You came looking and now you have it and more."

His voice twisted into a sickening growl as her eyes rolled back, her lids fluttering, and she knew no more for a time.

It was cold. The air smelled of wet leaves and of rich humus lying just beneath them. Her back ached, her legs ached, and her mouth felt as though it had been wiped with ashes.

Melisse sat up, opening her eyes to see the clearing where she had encountered the young man. There was no one now but her.

Her head ached as she crawled about, gathering her clothing, the absurdity of what she had done this night coming back to her. She stood shakily, leaning against a sapling while dressing herself in the early morning light. Even her eyes hurt her against the dim light that had begun to show itself, although she knew that to anyone who had spent the night indoors it was still truly dark.

She began staggering back in what she thought was the direction of the manor house, even if the path was no longer there. She thought only of finding some small corner in the stables where she could sleep in soft straw and wait for dear Mathilde to come tell her that everything would be alright.

The two beings watched the young woman limp away. One of them chuckled.

"Such good sport. She really *was* unspoiled. I thank you for bringing her to me," he said.

The Will O' Wisp cocked an eyebrow at him, then said, "It was my pleasure. I doubt that the poor thing will ever enjoy an ordinary man after having been with you. A curious fate. As her first, you have surely marked her, and finding such…sensations…with anyone else will be quite impossible, I think."

"Oh please, Wisp, you're making me blush," he replied.

"There is one thing more, though," she continued. "I believe you gave her something there, just at the end. Something…interesting."

"You saw rightly," he conceded. "Do you mean a child? No, never that, but something to remember me by? Yes…I did. And we shall see just where that leads our sweet girl, now that she has something she can use before it comes to consume her."

He let out his breath then, and with a second sigh, he let fall the skin of the slops boy. His amber eyes were filled with fire and with a sound like that of breaking glass, the two slipped through a crack in the skin of the forest. Fire shimmered for an instant as they passed from one world to another, then both they and the doorway they had opened disappeared from view.

Her faltering steps strengthened as she worked her way through thick underbrush and up difficult terrain. At first she believed that she would bleed and had balled up one of her stockings in her undergarments, except that as she began to feel better and her muscles loosened, it seemed unnecessary.

She checked the stocking to find it quite dry and unstained. She continued walking back through the darkness, trying to avoid thinking of the smell of smoke that clung to her like shame.

Her strength continued to return and soon Melisse began to make good time, believing that she would be back to the manor in half the time it had taken to follow the path the night before.

She stopped to get her bearings, unused as she was to finding her way in the outdoors. She put her hand on a young larch to hold herself steady on the slope of a small hill when she smelled smoke again, only much stronger this time.

Suddenly she was sure that she had come upon some woodsmen cutting timber for Lord Perene's hearth. Perhaps they were camped nearby, their fire burning fall leaves, producing that unmistakable odor.

She strained her ears, listening for voices or other sounds to indicate where the woodsmen might be. The forest was dreadfully silent. As she peered about her, the odor of burning wood and leaves ever more present, Melisse saw a series of tiny fires smoldering upon the trail that she had taken.

Tiny fires, evenly spaced upon her path, the span of her strides apart. As the acrid scent of burning bark lifted in the air, she jerked her hand back from the larch, crying out at the sight of its burning wood, blackening where her hand had been.

Understanding came then as she looked back at the small regular fires, each smoldering in her footfalls as she blithely walked through the woods.

She saw him again, holding himself over her, growling like a beast with eyes flaming in amber, his cock pumping into her, pumping until she felt herself filled to overflowing.

Smoke continued to sting her eyes, and to her horror, she looked down and saw that the ground was burning where she stood.

She ran then, terrified of her own steps. The forest sped by, blurring as her tears burned, boiling away into steam as they ran down her cheeks.

He had done something to her. She had been cursed. There would be no returning to the manor, to the life she had always known.

She remembered his words as she came to stand, finally, at the edge of the manor's lawn. She reached out to rest a trembling hand upon a small tree and watched as it crackled and burned within her grasp. She had what she came looking for. She had made a choice and and had taken the path that led irrevocably away from the life she had always known.

She cried then, her tears steaming away in the early morning air. She lamented the demise of what had been laid out as her destiny from the moment of her birth as the child of a servant, who would live out a life of a servant and then die as a servant.

Her tears fell, but perhaps not all of them were in sadness. Melisse looked one last time at the facade of the manor, thinking of all the hearts beating behind its great stone walls, some subtle and cruel, others simple and kind, but none of them burning with the golden fire that filled her now.

She took strength from that thought and turned away, releasing the burning tree. She ran away from all of them and the life that had been hers. In the end, she found that it was not so difficult.

THE MARECHAL CHRONICLES: VOLUME 2, THE HUNTER

The interminable evening with Lord Perene had finally ended and the Marechal found his bedchamber quite comfortable, if not somewhat cold. He undressed quickly, down to bare skin, before he slipped between the many layers of quilts and blankets laid upon the baldaquin bed.

He blew out the candle at his bedside and stared in the darkness at the low red coals upon the grates of the fireplace. They had been hurriedly dumped there and not long ago. He doubted it would do much to warm the room and wondered mildly if he should have kept his shirt on.

Choosing not to move instead, he considered the words of Lord Perene earlier, just before the man's idiot son affronted the maidservant.

It would seem that I must read those passages written by Bellamere before I continue south, he thought. Details that would be of little notice, even to a collector accustomed to sifting through the words of rare texts, might be hidden in the recounting of the tale. Already there was the name of St. Lucq mentioned, and for that alone he determined that he must find some means of reading those pages. It would be delicate and would call for subtlety as Lord Perene would hold it over him, no doubt looking for some means of exacting a price. He would need to be prudent with his request. Or, perhaps, manage the thing without gaining their notice.

A small noise just outside his door drew his attention. The fine line of light from the corridor at the base of the door had begun to grow larger in tiny increments.

Then a diaphanous shape filled the doorway, making no sound, much as a phantom might move. Except that this phantom let out a small hiss upon stepping on the cold flagstone floor. The door shut behind it and it glided across the room before coming to rest at the Marechal's bedside.

Bemused, he said, "Helene. Have you come to check on the comfort of your father's guest?"

She replied, "Ah, you have not yet found sweet repose, dear Marechal. I fear that the room is too cold for a valued person such as yourself.

"Will you permit me to apologize?" she asked and then, without waiting for him to reply, her thin night robe dropped from her shoulders. In silhouette, he could see her rigid nipples and slim smooth waist just before she slipped under the quilts to lie beside him.

He said nothing as she nuzzled in close to him, bare skin upon bare skin. Hers was cool, dry, and soft in a way that reminded him of the ripe skin of an afternoon peach, freshly picked from the branch.

"Isn't this better, Marechal? I had thought to send the servants for a bed warmer of hot coals brought up from the kitchen ovens, but then I thought of a better solution, a more intimate answer to the chill evening air."

Her voice was softer than the blankets and she paused, waiting for him to fill in the moment, but he said nothing, nor did he move in the slightest.

Her hands found him and touched his chest, searching until she found the line of the scar that started at his jaw. She traced its lightning strike shape, lingering at his collarbone before continuing upward to caress his cheek.

She turned herself half over, draping a leg across his thigh. He could feel her downy hairs below brushing against his leg, promising warmth in its velvet confines. Her hand drifted back the way that it had come, her touch light across the muscles of his torso, still following the jagged track of a scar that did not seem to end.

With a brusque movement, he seized her wrist in a grip of iron. It was sudden and when she jerked back in surprise, she discovered that he did not move in the slightest, as if her wrist had been encircled by an oak that refused to bend in the wind.

"What do you want, Helene? I watched you this evening and could see the gears turning behind your eyes, all that you see caught up in the clockwork of your thoughts. I doubt that you do the least thing without some well considered motive."

She smiled, casting her eyes downward, demurring to answer for the moment. She turned away from him slightly, the loose curls of her coiffure slipping from their braided confinement. Her neck curved gracefully in a way that she knew men found captivating, supple and elegant in its charm.

The Marechal's grip loosened upon her wrist and she slipped smoothly from his grasp only to place her hand upon the well-defined muscles of his abdomen. There she found fine hairs that descended from his navel, coarsening and thickening under her searching fingertips, until she reached lower still, her fingers spread wide, to the hair between his legs, letting it fill the spaces between them.

She held him and he was rock hard, as rigid as his grip had been a moment earlier. He reached out to her, touching the outline of her side and the ribs that would show just under her silky skin. He brushed the side of her breast before taking it into the palm of his hand. She was not an overly endowed woman, a perfectly delicate equilibrium showing in her noble bloodlines. The light frame and structure of her body were reflected in her delicate breasts, tipped with small nipples. He had no doubt that in daylight they were champagne pink in color and that her breasts as exquisitely formed as the finest crystal goblet.

He rolled her nipple between his forefinger and thumb, thinking of how she had grown very still, even while holding him firmly in her hand under the quilts. She laughed lightly as he squeezed before she pushed his hand away.

She lifted up the quilts and then dived underneath them, her elegant body graceful in its every movement. The Marechal felt warm, humid breath before she closed her lips around him. Her tongue danced around the tip of his cock, light as a feather, from one side to the other in small circles that took his breath away. It was nearly too much and he had to steel himself from pulling back and away from her.

Sensing him and the tension in his legs, she changed the dance of her tongue, skipping as lightly as ever before coming to rest firmly under his head, where her tongue flattened and pressed against him with an amazing firmness before lifting up every so slowly in a long, single stroke that stopped short of the tip.

Despite his self control, his desire of self-mastery, the Marechal groaned in pleasure.

He felt her smile then, believing that she had won, before she took him entirely inside her mouth, descending in luscious full movements, accompanied by a tongue that danced as if fevered.

Her hand slipped around his sack, cupping him, then she held two fingers underneath it and pressed firmly. Inside her mouth she could feel him growing fuller under the pressure of her fingers, his tumescence heightening as she continued her fervent rhythm.

The Marechal reached out to her and ran his hand along the inside of her thigh, searching for the velvet hairs he had felt earlier. Finding them, he touched her lightly, only to find her cool and dry. In the same moment, she came to a sudden stop, her mouth suddenly less welcoming as she let her teeth rake down the side of his shaft. It was just short of unpleasant and the Marechal read the warning in her breath.

She twisted her buttocks from his grasp, then returned to the rhythm of her mouth upon him. She fondled his balls, returning her fingers to press again and again just below, where the root of his erection began before giving way to his anus.

What game is this? he asked himself, then decided that he would see it to the end.

Her tongue lapped at him and danced, and with a heave of his long thighs, the Marechal thrust himself into her mouth, matching her rhythm, daring her to back away. She came back at him with force and did not hesitate to take him even deeper.

The faint glow in the hearth had fallen down to mere embers while the two of them broke into a fine sweat. The elegant, fine lips of a noblewoman held him, and despite him, she was his match. She did not release him, nor did her tongue tire of the deep lapping strokes on the underside of his cock, until the Marechal could contain himself no longer, biting down hard, his jaw clenched, then the breath hissed out from between his teeth as the veins just under the skin of his hips lifted, as the motion of his abdomen stilled, tensing in the instant. He rose up off the bed, his back arched, and came hard into her mouth. He came like the lashes of a whip, striking out at the nobleman's daughter, yet she was his match and took all that he had to give.

She slipped out of the quilts, stooping lightly to the floor for her robe, and put it on before turning back to the Marechal.

"My father grows old and my brother is a fool, so our future falls to me and the small measures at my disposal. What I want is protection for my family…for my house, Marechal. You are an influential man, so I have offered what I have to give. I trust in your honor as a gallant man that you shall not forget it."

She padded lightly to the chamber door before letting herself out.

The coals in the hearth had fallen to ash. The Marechal frowned as he remembered her smile and the way it did not reach her eyes…even if he had to admit that he no longer felt the chill air.

A scream pierced the morning air, cutting it cleanly in two. The Marechal would have had some trouble saying whether it was a man or a woman, as high pitched the scream was in its horror.

He raced down the corridor, buttoning his trousers distractedly. The sound had not been far even if all had fallen deathly quiet in its aftermath. He turned a bend and saw a door ajar at the corridor's end. Just within were Lord Perene and his daughter, their faces ghostly white.

The Marechal stepped inside the bedchamber and saw the object of their attention. Lord Perene's heir, his son Olivier, was lying across a bed, his bare chest punctured by a number of wounds. The young man's eyes were wide and his face was locked in the rictus of pain of his final moments. The Marechal saw that he was as unmoving as a statue, all life fled.

His instincts as a man of the law of the realm began their inventory, methodically taking in the details he would need. He noted the small, bloody handprint on the doorframe, almost childlike except that it was positioned too highly.

He stepped closer to the bed as Lord Perene grated out, "Oh, my son…my poor boy." His voice was hoarse and strained. The Marechal thought the scream might have come from him.

"Who found him?" he asked.

There was a moment's hesitation as the normally poised Helene's eyes flicked to those of her father before the nobleman answered.

"My daughter did, Marechal. My darling Helene found her brother there, cut to ribbons."

She said, "We had planned to go riding this morning. I waited for him and thought that perhaps he'd overslept, so I came to wake him. And, I found him. Like this."

The Marechal saw that she was wearing what could be considered riding apparel, her skirt divided lengthwise in the current fashion of noblewomen preferring the control of the horse over customary sidesaddle riding. Besides this, he saw that she wore well made leather gloves, certainly appropriate for riding on a brisk autumn morning. Her eyes widened as his gaze went from her small, gloved hands to the bloody print at the door, but she said nothing, nor did she volunteer to take them off.

"Yes, yes…there, Marechal, at the door. Do you see it? There is all the answer you need. You saw her strike him last night. We both did. That low born scum slipped in here to cut my son down while he slept. Marechal, I demand that you do your duty." Lord Perene's voice shook with emotion.

The Marechal said nothing while he took his time, looking about the room, taking it all in before turning to look pointedly, unblinking, at both the young woman and her father.

"Well, what is it, man?" asked Lord Perene in exasperation.

"Nothing," replied the Marechal, "for now…"

The dew was still sparkling on the lawn as the Marechal stepped out the kitchen's back door. The woman behind him, heavyset and kindly, held a towel in her hands and twisted it in her worry for Melisse. She had told him that she had last seen Melisse when she had sent her to empty the slops in the pig's enclosure. That she had been told to spend the night in the stables afterward, until Lord Perene calmed himself.

Except that the maidservant never arrived in the stables. None of the manor's staff had seen her after Mathilde had sent her on her way.

The Marechal walked the flagstone path that wound around to the back of the manor house. At a bend in the path, he saw a large kettle on the ground. Coming closer, he saw that it was full of vegetable peelings and other castoffs from the kitchen.

Strange, he thought, why leave this here, unless...

He looked about him and then remarked the fine trace of footsteps that had pressed down the grass, dimly visible upon the dewy lawn. Following them, the Marechal walked to the wooded edge of the lawn's limit. As he stood there, he heard a shout and saw Lord Perene come stomping toward him, rigid in anger.

The Marechal ignored him as he looked around, searching for some further sign of the servant. Seeing nothing else, he followed the forest's edge, thinking that he would circle around before heading into the trees on the trail of Melisse.

He did not have far to go before he saw a small pine with a blackened patch on its trunk. The breath hissed out of him as he drew closer to the tree just as the nobleman arrived behind him.

"Why aren't you on your horse pursuing that filthy woman? I tell you, I want her head!" he shouted.

And then Lord Perene saw what had drawn the Marechal's attention. A handprint branded into the bark of the tree. The small handprint of a woman.

"Witchcraft! A witch has been hiding in my household and now has killed my son!" he screeched. The Marechal was more than ever convinced that the scream that had awakened him this morning came from the father and not the daughter.

"You'd do well to calm yourself, sir. As you say, I am bound to my duty. Leave me to it, then."

The Marechal cast about him, looking for anything else that might help in finding Melisse when what he next saw took his breath away.

At the base of the tree were footprints burned deeply into the ground as if it had been done with a glowing hot iron and not the soft tread of a young servant woman.

It was plain before him as he followed the burnt steps that led across the manor's lawn. The grass had been crisped and was blackened down to the soil. They led south and as he followed them, the stride of the branded footsteps lengthened more and more in what he understood to be someone who had broken into a run.

Only, the distance between each footfall swiftly grew to inhuman proportions, lengthening the span between them until finally there was one last burnt step in the grass and then nothing else. The Marechal cast about him, walking a broad arc while sweeping his gaze from side to side. Except that it seemed as though whoever had made those branded footsteps had simply vanished.

Turning to the nobleman, he said, "Lord Perene, please have my horse saddled and laden with victuals for several days at least. It seems that I shall be cutting short my visit here."

He said it not without regret as he thought of Bellamere's text and the tantalizing details awaiting him just a short distance away in the manor's library. Details that would have to wait until his return.

"Yes, yes," said Lord Perene, "I ordered it done before even coming here to see what distracted you so. I felt sure that the wench would have fled and that there is no one more qualified than you to track her down."

The scar over the Marechal's jaw tightened and loosened as he chewed over his thoughts. He wanted each detail of his stay carefully etched in his memory.

A stableboy led his horse down to the two men, moving as quickly as he could.

The Marechal collected the reins before hoisting himself into the saddle.

"This will likely take some time, Lord Perene," he said, scanning the morning horizon. Then he turned the horse opposite the direction of the burned steps. He knew he would do best to cut cross country, avoiding most thoroughfares frequented by local travelers.

"Marechal!" shouted Lord Perene. "You're going the wrong way."

Pulling up, the Marechal called back to him. "As you say, Lord Perene, there is some witchery at work here and to take up its path, I am in need of aid."

The nobleman marched up to him once more. "But my hounds are at your disposal, sir."

"Your hounds would avail nothing, Lord Perene. The aid I seek lies to the north, even if I am loathe to seek it.

"However, I *shall* hunt her down. I shall do my duty as Marechal de Barristide. And I promise you, Lord Perene, I shall come back here, with the truth at the heart of this affair firmly in my grasp. I promise that justice at my hand will fall without remorse upon the guilty."

The Marechal remarked with some satisfaction that Lord Perene had no answer to this, his face whitening under the Marechal's words.

The Marechal spurred his horse northward as he turned the morning over in his thoughts. There were details that troubled him, not the least of these was that Mathilde had told him that while she had not seen Melisse after sending her out to the stables, the kitchen woman had seen both Lord Perene and then his daughter come by to ask after Melisse that evening, as if concerned for her.

A servant woman's revenge. It seemed too easy for him as he thought of the nobleman and his daughter before the young man's deathbed, the two of them visibly shaken but dry-eyed just the same.

For now though, he had no choice. It had been a very long time since he had last seen *Her* and he had hoped that it would stay that way.

Except that *She* was his only hope of picking up the trail heading south, one that evaporated into nothing at the lawn's edge.

Despite himself and the morning sun warming him as he rode north, the Marechal shuddered. *She* was his only hope, but *She* had a price. And he knew it would cost him dearly….

The air crackled around her. To Melisse's ears it sounded like dry leaves trodden underfoot, only the sound was enormous, as if there were an entire army marching through a dying forest. She could see only dim shapes in an ash-filled darkness that obscured nearly everything. What she did see filled her with terror and she was thankful her vision was not clearer.

The heat that surrounded her was suffocating and she struggled to breathe. Only moments before she had begun to run across the manicured lawn of Perene Manor when the landscape around her had melted away in blurred, trembling relief. As the heat buffeted her, she could not help but think that it was like looking from within an inferno toward the exterior of an unburnt world.

The heat mounted until finally, when she thought she could bear it no longer, there was a sound of breaking glass. The world shattered around her, the shards of it falling into place, a mirror breaking in reverse. Color and sound flooded in to fill her senses. Soft ground then underfoot, she breathed blessedly cool evening air, drinking it in like spring water.

She was on a wooded hillside and she knew that she had come far, even if she did not know how. Through burning fires that ebbed and flowed within her, of that she was sure, but she knew no more than this.

For the moment though, it seemed that the heat had calmed within her. Her feet did not burn the ground beneath her and she no longer scented smoke and ash with each inhalation.

Across the small valley before her, she saw a farmhouse and just behind it, a barn. Thinking of Mathilde, Melisse thought that passing the night nestled warmly in straw was more interesting than huddling against a tree in the open air.

There was candlelight flickering in the farmhouse, but she managed to slip by unremarked, making no sound. The barn door's well-oiled hinges did not creak as she eased it open. Within were housed two horses and an ass, but they seemed to take no interest in her. Only the horses whickered softly as she climbed a ladder to the loft above.

It was piled high with clean fresh straw and Melisse wasted no time in finding herself a likely spot, well away from the ledge that opened upon the barn floor below. She swept out a hollow with her hands then lay upon the soft straw. Its smell was dry and good, reminding her of harvests and laughing farmers. It was with these thoughts that she forgot the golden flames hiding within her and she slipped away into an innocent young woman's dreams.

The whickering of horses. A gentle sound of calm recognition. The rungs of the ladder creaking under the weight of someone. These were the sounds that lifted Melisse up from sleep and filled her with dread. Her heart hammered in her chest as she did her best to quietly sink lower into the straw.

The creaking stopped and all was silent for a moment before a low chuckle broke the quiet.

"You've done well, hiding yourself deep as you did…except that you forgot one of your feet. It's sticking up, proud as can be, but I think it's likely attached to someone all the same."

His voice held no anger and for that Melisse sighed with relief. She sat up and raked straw from her hair while a young man on the ladder opened the visor of an oil lamp. She blinked, reminded of the bobbing light that had lured her away from her quiet life in the manor into passion that burned all in its wake. She recoiled from him despite knowing that this was not the same young man that she had encountered in the forest.

He looked puzzled and then made a sort of clucking sound with his tongue. She thought it a strange thing to do and then realization broke and she laughed out loud.

"So, you would calm me as you calm your horses?" And because it was so surprising and genuine of him, she laughed out loud again, delighted.

He took his turn at being flustered, and then because there was nothing else to do, he laughed with her as he climbed over the ladder and into the loft.

"You went by so quiet, I could have sworn it was a cat. I was outside on the stoop of the front door, admiring the night sky when you came ghosting along. I near didn't see you until you turned to look back and I saw the moon flash in your eyes.

"That's why I was reminded of a cat. That golden flash that shined in the darkness before you crept away to hide in our barn."

She whispered, "I'm sorry. I know I shouldn't have done, but it was late and it seemed best not to bother anyone with asking if I could. In case you were sleeping, I mean."

"Oh, I see," he whispered back. "That was very polite of you. To think of not waking anyone. Very polite.

"But can you tell me something? And please, think before answering because I believe it's very important. Can you tell me why we are whispering?"

He said it with such perfect solemnity that she caught herself wondering exactly why and how to explain it well when he laughed again with that low chuckle that tugged at Melisse, deep in her belly.

"Well, you said 'our', so I was whispering to be quiet for quiet's sake," she replied, indignant.

He rolled his broad shoulders, watching her intently, and she was reminded once more of the young man in the forest.

He said, "For now, there is no 'us' or 'our'. My father loaded up a wagon full of potatoes to sell in the city south of here. I stayed behind, alone, seeing as there is no one else but me and him here to take care of the animals and keep wandering strangers out of the barn.

"Turns out, I'm only good at half those things," he said.

She sighed. "I, too, know what it is to be alone. I never knew my father and two years ago a fever took my mother during the harsh winter."

"My own mother died when I was just a little boy," he replied. "She passed while giving birth to twins, my brother and sister. Her gone and the two never arrived, leaving just my father and me."

The two of them fell silent, thinking, but both at ease in the moment with the scent of straw in the air as they watched tiny particles of dust gently spinning in the light of the lantern.

The young man cleared his throat and said, "So, I'll bid you a good night, dear lady." He made to get up from his place in the straw and before Melisse could consider what she had to say, she blurted, "No. Don't go. Please."

He sat back down slowly.

"I mean, if you don't want to, you don't have to go," she mumbled even as she slid closer to him.

She leaned in close to him, surprised with her own daring, letting her breast push gently against his arm. She smelled the scent of youth and soap upon him, the odors of hard work washed away even as his manhood ran just beneath the surface.

He cleared his throat again and Melisse could feel him trembling slightly even if he did not move away from her.

"How old are you?" she asked in a whisper as she came close to his ear. She wanted to drink his odor in and hoped to hear again that low laugh that reached down and pulled at her insides.

"I've seen twenty summers," he said, swallowing as he did it.

She could see a fine bead of sweat breaking out on his forehead and color beginning to shine in his cheeks.

"Have you known a woman, yet?" Her voice had taken on a throaty tone, one that Melisse almost could not recognize. She only knew that she felt alive, fully alive, and that the young man beside her was suddenly the most fascinating thing she could imagine.

He swallowed again and she watched the quick rise and fall of his throat. His skin was unflawed and deeply tanned. His shoulders were heavy and square within his shirt and she knew that his life on the farm had been good to him. Well-nourished, his muscles were as developed as any young stallion in the stables of Perene Manor, shining, quivering, ready for explosive action.

Without waiting, without caring for his answer, Melisse was overwhelmed in her thirst for him. His skin held secrets that she had to discover. No longer interested in how she found the courage, she came at him, slipping her tongue along his jawline before taking his lips within her own. She took in his surprised gaze as she kissed him deeply, his eyes opening even wider as she forced her tongue into his mouth. She held him and then, breaking contact with his mouth, she forced herself against him, lifting up and pressing her breasts against him.

"Never," he whispered, trembling.

She did not reply, taking hold of his arms instead. She eased them up and placed his hands upon her ample breasts, then she guided his fingers over her chemise to her nipples.

"Pinch them," she gasped.

He did, but very lightly, as if afraid he would hurt her.

"No, harder…please," she said.

He did once more, but with almost no change. A flame of anger and frustration bloomed in Melisse as she lashed out at him.

"No! I said harder, or you'll wish you had."

He flinched, but then gripped her nipples and gave each a wrenching pull. The pain of it only inflamed Melisse further as she brought her legs around him before easing down to place her crotch tightly against his own. The hardness she felt through his trousers promised much.

He rolled her nipples between his fingers, squeezing them tightly, until it felt as though the tips of her breasts were on fire.

Melisse leaned back, pulling her shirt over her head without bothering to unbutton it. The young man, seeing the challenge in her eyes, did the same, a grin spreading across his face as he saw Melisse's chest in the light of the lantern. Her nipples were dark and erect, the breasts themselves swollen in her excitement.

The young man reached down and with fumbling fingers undid his belt and trousers, sliding them down and kicking them off hurriedly.

His penis wagged back and forth as he moved back against Melisse who watched him, her eyes shining in the darkness.

She pushed her skirt down and off her hips, then she rose up before him as she stepped clear of it. The shadows painted her in half silhouette but he could see the darkness between her legs. The scent of musk was in the air and his nostrils flared involuntarily with it.

"I saw the moon flash in your eyes," he said. "Except that there was no moon. The clouds had covered it over. I think I am dreaming this, of you, an imaginary creature."

She replied, her voice strong and husky, "I am real."

She took his hand and brought it between her legs where she was all heat and heaviness.

"*This* is real."

She released him but he kept his hand where it was, stroking her, letting his fingers explore her folds, finding the small hardness that lifted up out of the softness there. She arched her back, groaning.

"You are so warm," he whispered.

A sense of warning flashed within Melisse. A small voice tried to make itself heard only to be drowned out by the mounting heat of her desire. Her hips tilted and pushed against the young man's probing touch.

His fingers slipped inside her, pushing in deeply, brushing and stroking. The heat grew within her.

In a sudden movement, she pulled back from him and then threw herself down on all fours, panting.

"Put it in me," she breathed. "Like a dog, oh, put it in me."

The young man quickly obliged her, gripping her hips from behind and eased himself inside after fumbling only a little. She was sure he knew what he was about due to his life on the farm. He pushed in hard as she thrust herself back upon him, spearing herself.

"Do it, do it, do it," she panted as she slapped at his well-muscled thigh.

He pulled back and thrust forward and she heard that low chuckle once more. She imagined he was smiling in his pleasure as he pistoned into her, gaining force with each thrust. Together they moved against each other, the flesh of her buttocks rocking as his hips slapped into her over and over again.

And then, inexplicably, he gasped out, "The moon…"

He seemed to turn perfectly rigid behind her, his cock quivering, before he seized the flesh of her haunches and slammed into her as she felt him spraying deep inside her, pumping into her. Pumping into her like the man in the forest.

The heat lifted up in a single crackling moment and engulfed her. Melisse strained against it, reaching out, searching for the young man orgasming inside her, but her hands found nothing as everything turned to golden flame and rippling heat.

As through a fog, she heard the susurration of crackling autumn leaves, and behind that, as if from very far away, there were the sounds of horses screaming.

She felt flames ripping at her, gnawing at her flesh, searching for purchase. It was a wild beast that had lain in wait, slyly watching, gauging the moment when it could leap up and sink it golden claws into her, its prey.

Melisse understood then that it had been an illusion. The illusion of another life, no longer a servant, ready to find some other destiny in the world. She had been wrong to think that she could break away from the fate that had been stamped upon her even as she slipped, wet and bloody, from between her mother's thighs into the world.

That she would always submit to the will of others. That she would have no say in her life, nor in her death. That she would submit one final time as a servant submits to the desires of her master.

The golden flame that had hidden inside her stretched out its talons, ready and hungry to tear into her servant's flesh, desiring only to burn her life away in its blind greed to consume.

Melisse bowed her head, taking a deep breath that seared her lungs. She let the flames approach as she felt herself become small, ordinary, ready to be effaced as if she had never existed.

Then, at first very quietly, in nearly a whisper, she said, "No."

The fire ignored her, bearing down upon her with all the weight of its heat and flame.

She said, "No," again, and began to repeat herself, each time growing louder and louder.

The flame recoiled at her refusal then burst forward again, curling itself around her. Melisse thought she could hear laughter in the hissing flames.

She opened her arms wide and said, "No, you shall not destroy me. I accept what you are and take you back inside me. You cannot destroy yourself as it is I who consume you."

She hurled her will, her endless intransigence, her strength to endure all that had ever come to press down upon her servant's heart, she took it all and forced the fire back and back, turning itself around and upon itself.

It fought against her, screaming in burning rage, but Melisse only held herself against it, her obstinacy her rock, her implacable will her shield. And in the end, sensing that mastery was hers, Melisse released it.

The flames burst forward against her like a lightning strike, vicious and terrible in its fury. Melisse opened herself against it and as it struck, she took it inside herself, took all of its savagery and made it part of her. She accepted it, opening herself as she had done when spreading her thighs in the forest. She gave it the admittance that was hers to give, willingly becoming its servant. And in so doing, she became its master.

The barn was burning down around her. Sheets of flame leapt up from the walls and the intense heat buffeted against Melisse but it could not harm her. Her own flame filled her and its golden hue had turned the rich red of the blood coursing through her body. As she descended from the loft and stepped over the threshold, the yellow fire of the burning building seemed but a paltry, mindless thing that shrank back from Melisse at her passage.

She turned to watch as the roof fell in and felt a pang of sadness for the young farmer and his animals. But there was a price to be paid, she knew, as she stood there, her clothing burned away, her skin flawless and burnished in the golden flame that had come to consume her.

She searched the sky, looking for the moon. She thought she might wish that the young man's spirit find its way there. But the clouds kept it for themselves and hid it away.

She turned to look across the dark land and she smiled, her eyes flashing a rich red gold. She had paid a price and it had been dear, but the mastery of her destiny was hers now, and of that, she was glad.

Castor was not happy. They were camped on the trail they had found earlier that afternoon. Their wagon was loaded to overflowing with cut wood for the hearths of Perene Manor and he had been for pressing onward, even if it meant flogging the horses forward in the darkness of the night.

Burnt footprints. It was worse than a bad omen and he wanted only to be on his way home.

"Come on, Castor. Have some stew, man," said Willem. He held out a heel of hard bread and nodded to the cast iron pot at the edge of the campfire.

"I'm not hungry," said Castor, "And nor should you be."

"Oh garn, Castor. Don't let a few silly footprints spoil yer dinner."

Willem was younger than him by ten years and did not hold with superstition or the tales they had all heard at their grandmother's knees. For Willem, they were but stories to pass the time and nothing more. Castor knew better.

"Where's Frederic?" he asked Willem.

"He left when you went to hobble the horses. He's gone back with a lantern, looking for the direction of those tracks through the woods. Garn! What a strange thing to find out here."

In all Castor's years as a woodsman, he had never seen such a thing. And he hoped never to see it again, the mere idea of it filling him with dread.

"You two are fools," grated Castor. "We should'a kept on goin', right up to our own doorsteps without stoppin'. That burnt trail there means nothing but bad, I tell ya."

A strangely musical sound of breaking glass interrupted him. It was as if hundreds of bottles had come crashing down, shattering themselves upon a great heap in the depths of the forest.

Castor looked past Willem, peering into the darkness that followed the trail they had found.

Willem had begun to turn back to Castor, a wide smile on his lips, when Castor heard the sound of feathered wings beating. It was a soft sound, like an owl's wing beat, except that it sounded as if there were hundreds of them. Over Willem's shoulder, Castor caught a glimpse of feathers and of eyes swiftly flying along the trail of burnt footsteps, hundreds of rainbow colored eyes, and without thinking, he threw himself backward, flat upon the bare ground.

In the instant that it took the thing to flap across the clearing, Castor saw Willem's head tip from his neck in a flurry of blinding white plumes to fall down, rolling like a stone kicked loose on a hillside. Castor had an instant to think that Willem did not even know he was dead as he watched Willem's smile roll with his head, his eyes twitching from side to side.

Castor flipped himself over, cast a glance behind him, and then leaped to his feet, running for all he was worth out of the clearing.

The horses snorted behind him and then he heard them screaming before coming to a sudden stop.

He lengthened his stride, no longer caring if he might catch his foot in a hidden root that would throw him down with a broken leg. He was suddenly sure that that it no longer mattered.

He heard it again, that gentle sound of many wings beating, muffled in a way that should have been comforting. And then he saw the forest spin in a long, lazy circle as cool air encircled his neck. Before the light of his eyes dimmed entirely, Castor had time to wonder at the white wings and the sight of so many rainbow eyes. There was a flute-like sound, musical and heartbreaking, and he thought to himself that his grandmother had been wrong…that this was what angels must look like and it was a terrible thing to behold.

His horse picked her way carefully through the snaking roots of the willow trees that surrounded them. The Marechal hated swamp country, always dark under the canopy of thick leaves, secrets hiding under the surface, all of it lurking and dangerous.

He had ridden hard to the north, pushing his horse as fast as he dared. He knew that the trail the servant girl had left behind would fall cold very quickly, but he had no choice. If he expected to find the footfalls of someone who had disappeared into thin air, he must appeal to powers beyond his own reckoning.

There, enshrouded in mist with long trails of moss hanging from its eaves, was the house. It tilted crazily to one side, threatening to upend itself into the murky water of the swamp. Except that it appeared to have always been that way. The Marechal imagined it was a caprice of the proprietor, a sort of sign to those who wandered upon the place by chance and not by purpose. Pass on, it said, or risk your doom.

He would have very much liked to pass on by the house. Instead, he dismounted and tied his horse well. She was a sturdy, brave animal, but even the most courageous horse could be startled off to find itself mired and drowning in the fog. The swamp remained a dangerous place for man and beast alike.

The front door of the crazily leaning house creaked open as he approached. The sound was like mice squealing, caught in some horrid trap.

But no, it is I, the mouse which walks willingly into the trap, he thought as he stepped inside.

The door creaked closed behind him.

The smell of rot and years upon years of layered dust hung in the air. The Marechal stood still and listened, waiting to hear the faintest sound of a floorboard under someone's heel.

Instead, he felt the fine hairs at the back of his neck tickle as a cool draught of air stirred behind him.

He whirled around, drawing his sword and taking a full step back in a single fluid motion. Poised, ready to lunge and strike a killing blow, he saw her. Her black robes were in tatters and a moth-eaten veil covered her head entirely. Where her left arm should have been, there was only an empty sleeve dangling. In her right hand, her yellowed nails curled round the head of a twisted tree root upon which she leaned heavily.

He could not see more in the dim light, and for that, he was glad.

"So, the Marechal de Barristide…I believe that is the name you use now," she croaked.

"The Marechal has come to pay a visit. How nice." She pushed past him with a crooked gait, knocking his drawn blade aside as if it were a child's toy. The Marechal grimaced at the odor of an old woman's sweat and grime as he sheathed his weapon.

"Yes, witch. And I have not come to bandy words about with you in the guise of pleasantries. Etiquette has no place in this abode of shadow and ill intention."

"Guard your tongue, Marechal," she said, twisting his title bitterly in her mouth. "Those closest to the Alchemist would have never used such a tone with me. You'd do well to remember that."

"The Alchemist?" he stuttered. "What do you know of him? What can you tell me?"

"What can *I* tell *you*?" she said, turning about to peer directly at him. Slowly, she reached up and lifted a corner of her veil. The Marechal flinched at the wizened face from which a single yellow eye, shot through with swollen, red blood vessels, stared out at him. The other half of her face remained mostly hidden, but he thought he saw that half of her visage was missing, as if torn away, the remaining flesh puckered and raw.

"You've been addled…I see," she muttered before letting her veil fall back down.

"What I can tell you is that he was successful, Marechal," she said. "More than this, though, requires payment."

She limped away from him with dragging footsteps. The Marechal had no choice but to follow.

The room they entered was one from tales meant to frighten children, tales meant to quell the worst behaved. There were rickety shelves lining the walls and upon those shelves were dust ridden bottles and jars, many of which had had their lids eaten through with rust, their contents slumped in drying sludge.

The Marechal dropped his gaze from them and their hideous reserves. In some, he was sure to have seen the corpses of the unborn and that alone was enough to force his gaze aside.

"But I doubt that you came with the intention to pay for more than one boon, Marechal," she said.

"No," he replied. "It is already too much. Although my memories remain jumbled, I knew where to find you and that you could accord me an answer to my needs."

"And that there be a price?" she asked.

"Yes, of that, too, I know," he said, wishing once again that he had never come to her door.

"Of the Alchemist, you have not sought me out. No, but you do seek yet another, yes?"

"You see truly, witch. I must find a woman implicated in the murder of a nobleman. A woman who may also be able to shed some light upon other deaths of a nefarious sort."

The bent, old woman turned to search among her affairs, small bottles and vials clinking as her single twisted hand sorted through them.

"A mere woman? The famed Marechal de Barristide needs my aid for so little?" she said, the amused sarcasm not at all veiled in her voice.

He replied, "A woman whose trail, from one step to the next, vanishes without a trace. There is some power at work and that it is at the heart of other dark deeds, I am nearly certain."

"That is why I have come," he finished.

She turned back to him, a tiny, dark blue bottle in her hand. She held it out to him and said simply, "My price, Marechal."

He took it from her gingerly, taking care not to touch her yellowed skin and grateful that whatever the bottle contained, there was mercifully little of it. He did not hesitate and unstoppered it quickly before upending the contents into his mouth. He swallowed forcefully, all the while holding his breath, expecting the worst.

Instead, the thick solution seemed to pool in the back of his throat, at once sweet and cold. He took a breath and in that moment, the liquid lifted up in a vapor that filled his lungs full. It was as though he had had a breath of frigid mountain air, or of winter distilled.

The old woman chuckled and said, "Good…good. And now, I would like to introduce you to my daughter. You see, we have so few visitors, she would be disappointed if she could not spend some time with such a handsome man. Such a *young* man…"

The Marechal had no words with which to respond. His tongue was frozen in place, as were his limbs. He found that he could not move even his smallest finger as the old woman hobbled from the room.

The light grew dimmer until he could no longer see the shelves across from him. He saw only that he was alone in the faint glow of a circle and that it now appeared as if the walls had receded, with dark nothingness taking their place. Even the faint sounds of the swamp outside the witch's house were gone. The constant drip of water, the raucous cry of some distant bird…all of it had dwindled to a muffled silence.

The Marechal had begun to wonder if the drink had somehow stoppered his ears when he heard a female voice, low and silky, speak from the surrounding shadows.

"Oh, you lovely man," he heard her say. He saw her emerge from the darkness and into the pool of light surrounding him. First came one long bare leg, the flesh of a marble purity that would have taken his breath away if he had not already been spelled still.

The rest of her followed.

She was dressed in gauzy transparent black, a sort of robe such as noblewomen wear, except that the hemline was ragged, running in deep zigs and zags that showed the Marechal tantalizing glimpses of firm white skin before being hidden away again as she moved with a delicious languor around him.

Her hair was long, black, and shone like the finest silk, as if she had magicked the glint of fine silver into her color. Her lips were luscious and full, of a red deep and profound. The color reminded the Marechal of heart's blood running down the length of his sword, the final beats of his opponent's life felt down to the pommel.

She was carnal, she was feline. Dark and light, she was contrast in motion.

Despite his compromised circumstances, the Marechal felt himself respond, his member growing heavy and warm, lengthening as he felt his pulse descend into his crotch.

"What an interesting scar, Marechal," she said. Her finger lingered at his jaw, tracing down to come round to his shirt front where she lightly flicked the buttons.

She leaned in close, letting her lips brush against his ear, and asked breathily, "Do you want me…Marechal?"

He felt his throat unlock with a hitch. He swallowed, then said, "What I do or do not want seems to be irrelevant at the moment. I believe that is the game we are playing, no?"

"Oh, this is no game, Marechal," she replied. "I am deadly serious. My intentions for you have nothing of goodness in them.

"My love for visitors is in their suffering, which can be so poignant, so exquisite…so charming."

She stepped away from him and he saw that she carried a cavalier's quirt in her hand. In a long drawn out motion, she drew her hand back and then swung at him, lashing his chest with what he believed was her full strength.

There was a crack and he felt the venomous sting of the lash leap through him. He clenched his jaws around the sound threatening to escape, sweat springing to his brow.

He fought against it, but he could feel that his erection had become enormous, straining against his trousers.

"Do you want me?" she asked again, her voice low as she reached out to toy with the tear in his shirt that the quirt had left behind. Her finger came away red and she licked his blood from it, smiling.

"That taste. It is amazing, Marechal. You really are of a special vintage, aren't you?

"You must make women weak in the knees and loose in the hips with the slightest glance. They take in your muscled shoulders, that broad chest hiding inside your immaculate white shirt. You come to them with thighs of oak and iron and lower yourself down upon them, letting them feel the weight of a real man, a man in his prime, rich, cultured, as you mesmerize them with your gray gaze and long lashes.

"Why I should imagine they are ready to come with just a smile from you, Marechal. Your beautiful smile as yet unstained by time or by wine."

The Marechal said nothing, the lash on his chest pulsing with each beat of his heart. He could feel small runnels of blood leaking down across his abdomen. And still, he felt that he had become enormously, preposterously aroused.

She walked behind him and with no warning, she struck him again, two vicious cracks echoing in the air. His back felt as though he had just been gored by a bull, the pain so intense that he gasped with the suddenness of it.

He knew she was goading him, but that knowledge did not stop his anger from blossoming into red rage.

With his most mighty effort, he summoned his strength, willing his arms to move. In that moment, as the blood coursed down his back, he wanted this woman's neck in his hands, wanted to see fear in her eyes as he held her life between forefinger and thumb.

He roared like a wild beast, but his arms only twitched loosely, the geas of the spell holding him. He smiled inside though. A twitch meant that he could weaken the spell's hold, he could work against it, and in time, break free.

"And you are a fighter as well, my dear," she said, amused. Something in her tone troubled him.

"But you shall not have the time you require, Marechal."

With a jerk, he felt his trousers come undone and then she was pushing at his back. His body obeyed her touch as he was forced to bend over. She slapped the quirt against the inside of his thighs and to his horror, he spread his legs wide.

"Oh, so much better. If only you could see the look on your face," she said as she circled around him, trailing her fingertips upon his back.

Coming to a stop behind him, the Marechal felt the quirt touch lightly at his anus. He tried desperately to tighten, to find some means of stopping what she was about to do, but he was powerless.

There was pressure and then there was pain at the unfamiliar sensation. He felt suddenly full, deep cramps racking him as he heard her laughter from behind him.

"Don't you like that, dear?" she asked as she walked around to his front. He could still feel the quirt where she left it, pushing at his insides.

She pushed lightly at his shoulders, forcing him back up to a standing position. She took his penis in her hand, pulling and pushing, as the quirt behind him dangled and swung with her movements.

The Marechal groaned. It was a melange of pain and pleasure. It was not new for him, not after all this time, but to be held powerless in the face of it, a plaything for the whims of another was altogether different and worse than unsettling.

"Calm yourself, Marechal. I can see my toy twitching back there," she chuckled. Then she dropped to her knees before him and enveloped his cock with her lips. The heat of her mouth was intense and she pressed her tongue tightly against him as she worked up and down his shaft.

He wanted to refuse her, to break her hold upon him. Instead, the sensations that he felt overwhelmed him. He could feel the quirt rocking inside, pushing against him with a steady rhythm in time with the motions of the woman as she took him deep into her mouth with full, zealous strokes.

The most profound muscles of his abdomen began to tighten and he could feel himself lifting up, his cock stiffening in its extremity. In great shuddering breaths, he came into her mouth, his muscles spasming, the sensations arising as much from the flesh holding the quirt in place as from the base of his member, pulsing with the force of his orgasm.

The Marechal strained, heaving and heaving, his muscles rippling in the throes of the moment even as his vision dimmed to near darkness.

Then she was upon him and he, suddenly flat on his back, could only watch as she sank down over his cock, her pendulous breasts now bared and her nipples standing out in reddened fury.

"I have never known the pleasure of riding a horse, Marechal," she said while she slid up and down his cock. "But I imagine it is like this, and that at times, you must show the beast who is master."

She held the quirt up high where he could see it before bringing it down behind her to strike against his exposed thighs. She lashed him again and again until it felt as though he had caught fire and was burning alive under her undulating hips.

Worse still, he remained as rigidly erect as ever and felt himself growing fuller with each lash at her hand. The pain lifted his cock higher into her even as his sack drew itself up tight, readying for the inevitable.

"And in time," she panted as she rode him relentlessly, up and down, "...the beast learns to like it, helpless, even as he burns in hatred."

And the Marechal recognized the truth of it. He hated her to the very depths of his being even as she flogged him to orgasm, the climax erupting into her, his body arched involuntarily against her. She dropped the quirt and pushed herself down tightly over him as he filled her. Her smile peeled back her lips and the Marechal saw in her eyes the reflection of dull, blurred death. He felt his member surrounded, as if by fingers, as it was pulled and sucked from within, as if she was desperate for every last drop of him.

The orgasm rocked through him over and over until even his teeth chattered through his clenched jaws.

When finally he had nothing more to give, she released him and leaned back, looking at his face. She could see hatred and lust burning in his gray eyes, violence quivering in his flesh.

She laughed then, laughed with the voices of the swamp, the sound of endlessly dripping water and the hoarse cries of waterfowl come to sieve their prey from the murk. She laughed as the dreary room of shelves resolved themselves before the Marechal's eyes, even as she drifted away in tendrils of mist scented with twisted desires and vile motives.

The Marechal found himself standing upright and lifted his arms to find his shirt unblemished and his trousers in place. He let out a long breath, easing his head from side to side, before clenching his hands into fists. If he could, he meant to find the woman and pay her back in kind.

Instead, the witch stood across from him, cackling softly from beneath her veil.

"My daughter shall treasure this moment with you, Marechal...oh yes, treasure it she will for many years to come," she said.

The Marechal slowly unclenched his hands and asked, "That I might return the favor to her is now a very dear wish. Where shall I find her when the moment is due, witch?"

The old woman snickered. "She's right there, in front of you," she said, waggling her stick at the shelves beside her. Toward the jars of the unborn, floating in their viscid juices.

"Of course, I have several daughters, Marechal. Finding the right one is another thing altogether," she continued, finishing with a cackle.

The Marechal thought he saw one of them move ever so slightly, and he shuddered.

"The price is paid, witch," he said. "Aid me now, or you will wish you had never heard of me."

She did not move for some time and the Marechal thought that she might have lost her wits with the weight of her age so heavily upon her. But then she stirred before reaching up to lift the corner of her veil clear from her one yellowed eye.

"I have already wished it, Marechal, year upon year…yet there you stand." Her voice had become small, quiet, human in its tone.

Then she turned as brusquely as her old woman's body would allow, fumbling once more at her innumerable bottles upon the shelves.

"Where is it?" she mumbled. She seized one of them in her gnarled grip and turned back to him.

"This will do, yes. We shall call upon those who might be of use to you, those willing, for a time, to share in your hunt for the woman."

With a sudden swing of her arm, she dashed the bottle to the ground where it exploded into fragments and dust. Instantly, a cloud of fuming smoke roiled up from the floor.

The witch called out in a language that set the Marechal's teeth on edge. Each word she spoke pulled at his guts with hooks of alien syllables and bizarre intonations.

Out of the smoke that clung to itself in a dense cloud, the Marechal heard what sounded like drums, their growing rhythm beating out a sound that resounded through the floor right to the soles of his boots.

With a crack and blaze of sulfurous light, the cloud bloomed and then fell down to form the long, low shape of a beast that must have measured seven feet long from snout to tail. It reminded the Marechal of a mixture of cat and lizard, although it carried itself on six short legs that ended in clawed talons. Its longitudinal trunk, rather like a log floating in the swamp, was carefully wound about in an intricately fashioned, silver chain, fitted like a mail shirt.

It peered up at him, blinking slowly first with one mud colored eye, then the other, before smiling wide with a mouth lined in sinister looking fangs.

"Strange," muttered the witch. "It is a Donglin. A redoubtable tracker...you could not have hoped for better. But that a demon such as this should have answered my call is very strange indeed."

"That you expected a lesser answer is of no importance. What matters is if I can have confidence in the fell beast," said the Marechal, his doubt plain.

The witch turned to the demon and although there were no words spoken, the Marechal felt that some sort of conversation was held.

"The demon seems to think that it is destined to serve you, Marechal. Although why, it will not say," she said, turning back to the Marechal."In any case, it gives its oath of fealty, which such as these do not give lightly.

"It will lead you to the girl unerringly, I believe, as the Donglin, once sworn to a cause, will never renege except in an encounter with its mortal enemy. And of that, there is little chance."

The Marechal asked, "How can you be so sure?"

"Their enemy since time immemorial is the Estril, beings of light and flame. Millennia ago and after near total decimation of the two races, they agreed to a truce. Never shall either race trespass into the other's domain. In this way, they have achieved peace between them.

"But should they encounter one another elsewhere, then by its very nature, the Donglin will forget all in its frenzy at the chance to exterminate an enemy upon neutral ground. However, that likelihood is remote. The Estril are a vain, haughty race, uninterested in the petty realm of mankind. The geas of the Donglin's oath will hold it to you, Marechal."

The Marechal looked doubtfully down at the demon, who had watched the witch during her discourse. If it had heard anything, the Marechal was unsure as he could see no ears upon the beast. But when she had finished, it turned its tooth-ridden smile back to the Marechal and quivered down its length. The Marechal could not help but be reminded of a dog anxious for the hunt.

"Does it know enough to hide itself when we cross paths with other travelers?" asked the Marechal.

"The Donglin has no need," she answered. "Demons of this sort are capable of avoiding undue attention. Except to the eyes of a person of real power, I should think most will see the illusion of a dog at your side and nothing more. A large dog, yes…but that is all."

The Marechal nodded.

"I have paid richly for the likes of you," he said to the Donglin. "Do not give me cause to regret it."

The old witch peered about her, then said, "Our dealings are done, Marechal. Begone with you. I grow tired of you. I grow tired of you and your misplaced past."

"That may be, witch," he said before striding over to the horrid jars. "But I promise that I shall not forget the repayment owed to her." He tapped his finger against one in particular, its lifeless occupant staring at nothing with its blurred, fishlike eyes.

In reply, the witch said, "My daughter is a willful child, to be sure. But the price you paid today,

Marechal, is a paltry thing against what I once paid in your very name. It is as nothing in comparison."

Her voice rising, she screeched, "Begone!"

Her hand wove some complicated figure in the air before she struck the floor with the heel of her twisted staff. The Marechal felt himself being pushed away even as the crooked house in the swamp receded from him, its lines squeezing down to nothing as the Marechal stood still upon mushy ground, his horse tied just behind him.

He hoisted himself astride his saddle then turned to cast an eye at the Donglin on the ground beside him.

"I travel swiftly, demon. Are you of a measure to keep pace with a tireless rider?"

The demon made no response other than to lift two rear legs clear of the ground on the side facing the Marechal. Well back and underneath, a dark opening lifted wide between the chain wrappings as an enormous, glistening blue penis slipped forward. It pushed out along the body of the demon until its thick blue head went past the demon's own face as it looked up to the man upon his horse. The smile it made then was a grin, in truth, as if to say that it was of a measure to anything.

The Marechal grimaced. "So be it. Now put that away, you foolish beast."

He turned his horse away from the mists swirling through the swamp before saying over his shoulder, "I think I'll call you…Blue."

The demon made no reply as it followed the man in unearthly silence, its grinning jaws filled with pointed insinuation.

THE MARECHAL CHRONICLES: VOLUME 3, THE PREY

S ilas heard voices. He was lying on what felt like a stone floor. There was warmth all around him and a golden light that bathed his environs, rendering him sightless. He could not be sure, but he thought he might have been blinded since all he could see around him shimmered and shifted in yellow tones.

"What is this, Lest?" he heard a man's voice say. The voice was hard, the exigence of whomever it belonged to clear in its clipped way of speaking. Silas could imagine that it was a soldier's voice, or at least, someone who held discipline in high regard.

"Raffiran, my darling!" A woman responded, her pleasure at the other's sudden appearance making her voice musical in tone.

"Oh this? It is nothing, dear," she continued.

"No, not nothing," the male voice said. "That is a man. A human."

There was a pause and Silas saw the colors before him ripple momentarily from rich yellows to a fleeting blue.

"I think I shall make of it my pet," she said. "You have your monster. Now I have this pretty man."

The male voice responded, "Lest, the point is not that you desire a plaything. Rather, I should like to know how you came by it."

Again, that shimmer to blue. Silas had always imagined blindness as an absolute darkness. An absence of all that made the world beautiful. Here though, he was immersed in a gold that he had seen once before, and not so long ago, reflected in the night eyes of a mysterious and beautiful woman.

"I found him only a little while ago," she said. "I felt my brother's magic bloom somewhere in the realm of men, so I reached out with all my strength, hoping to seize him, or at least to convince him to return to us before the Evangeline tracks him down.

"As Mesrin's fire burgeoned, I attempted to make contact. It was then that I perceived the presence of two beings, both human, one male, the other female. And in that moment, the female found some means to rebuff me. My brother's flame was perverted in some way and she pushed me back with a strength that was terrifying.

"I seized this man as she forced me away. My belief is that he may hold some clue to the mystery of that female and her link to my brother. Or at worst, this human shall make a pleasant diversion for me while you meddle in the affairs of men with your beast."

The male voice replied with a hard tone, rigid in its least intonation, "A human pushed you away? What mischief has your brother wrought in his foolishness?"

The male fairly growled as he continued.

"In any case, Mesrin shall be called to task shortly. My monster, as you call it, has scented his trail and its fury is swift, as always. If he resists, its answer shall be without mercy and our realm will be rid of his stupidity forever."

Deep red color bloomed before Silas's eyes, then receded in the unfathomable surroundings. He could not have said why, but Silas felt that the male presence had gone.

Then, with the fabric of color rippling before him, he understood that he had not been blinded after all. The form of a woman gathered itself out of the golden light. It was as though she walked forward, invisible, until she pressed against her own shape, like a bed sheet hung to dry, the outlines of her body lifting into view from nowhere.

Silas remembered the stories his father had told him of the great cities. His father had voyaged often in his youth before choosing the life of a farmer, the love he had for Silas's mother anchoring him at last. He had spoken of city temples devoted to strange gods and upon the great stepped terraces leading up to these edifices, his father had described magnificent statues rendered in the purest marble. He had said that the realism of them was more unnerving than anything those religions had shown him. The statues were of goddesses in the form of beautiful women, their perfection complete without flaw or error, and it was this that left his father in awe before the temples. He had had no need to mount the great stairs to see the mark of deities upon the world. It was there in those statues, and he understood that something of the divine had guided the hands of those who had created them.

Silas had never been to those cities, had never seen the great temples with their perfect sculptures. But here before him now, he saw all that his father had tried to describe for him. The woman standing above him as he cowered upon the hard floor was of a purity and perfection that spoke more clearly than anything that there was nothing of humanity about her.

Her voluptuous lips lifted into a smile that burned like fire in Silas's heart. She was nude and her narrow waist flared out in perfect proportions to hips that filled his vision. He tried to cover himself, horrified by the reaction of his body to the feminine glory before him now.

Her golden eyes, delicately almond in shape, shifted to regard his member lifting and lengthening. Full, round breasts tipped with stiffening nipples shifted deliciously as she watched his erection take form.

"Oh," she said, "We shall amuse ourselves to the fullest, my little man. And then you are going to tell me all about the woman...yes?"

Silas shivered. He knew that with this golden woman, there were no choices left to him.

She knelt down beside him and reached out to lift his chin in her hand. Her touch left his skin tingling as he looked into the golden orbs of her eyes.

"But first, you require some quickening. I doubt that your flesh could withstand me when my ardor mounts."

She held his chin and leaned forward to press her luscious lips against his. Silas felt her tongue slip forward and the taste of her was of spices that he had never tasted, of fruit that grows only in dreams.

His mouth tingled as she held him captive with her own. A deep flush of warmth rose in his chest, and without warning it was as though he drank fire. Flames slipped from the golden woman's mouth to slide down Silas' throat. They impaled him in a focused inferno and he could do nothing to break away.

The woman rocked her head back, breaking contact with him, and Silas took a great heaving breath. His throat felt as though it had been left in cinders as he swallowed fresh air. He could feel the warmth spread through his body and he had the impression that he became heavier, denser, as it enveloped him fully.

His skin tingled. Looking down at himself, he saw that his flesh, already deeply bronzed from his life as a farmer, had taken on some of the golden hue that infused everything around him.

"There," she said, "That should keep you from dying in my arms."

She was still on her knees and she pushed at Silas's chest, motioning that he should lie back flat upon the floor. The warmth of her flaming kiss ran through him still as he lay back. The hard surface seemed insignificant now, his flesh inured to minor discomforts.

Her breasts jostled in the most wonderful way as she slipped a leg over his torso to straddle him. He looked up and the two hills crested in thick points that called out to his mouth, the desire to suckle at her golden fount springing from his primal mind.

She moved further along his chest, to the point where his vision of her golden perfection was obscured, to the point where the heady scent of her musk filled his nostrils.

"And now, you will pleasure me, human," she said, the tone of her voice dropping a register, becoming husky and heavy as her scent filled his head.

Silas answered, "As you will, golden Lady."

A drop of her juices slipped down to patter onto his cheek and he craned his head forward, his mouth against her mound. His tongue ran out of his mouth of its own accord as he slipped it between her lips.

She tasted of salt and of roses. Her flavor was thick and it ran deep upon his tongue. He explored her folds, tasting here and there, desiring to know her every recess. And as she began to flex against his mouth in answer, he could hear her sigh with notes of melodic passion.

His experience with women was next to nothing, but of what little he had come to know ran counter to expectation. Silas had only ever known those who told him what to do and how to do it.

He pulled himself away from the gyrating hips of the golden woman. She thrust herself forward, her body demanding that he return to his ministrations. In answer, he flicked his tongue lightly at her lips, his touch fleeting. The woman laughed and the sound of her voice was filled with a smile that spoke to the flame now within Silas' flesh.

He smiled in return, no longer caring that he was subject to this woman's mastery. He would be hers, if she willed it. He teased her using his teeth, but gently so, then nuzzled in deeply, taking her as far as he could into his mouth. He sucked at her and her juices ran down his chin as she moaned.

The motion of her hips thrusting against him grew more intense. He strained to hold himself in place, to run his tongue up and down her cleft, pausing only to flutter at the hard point at her apex. Each time, he delighted in the way her rhythm would stutter in response before continuing again with a thrusting drive that grew in intensity.

When finally Silas was near to breaking, with his neck pinched in exhaustion, the woman panted before slapping forward hard against his lips. She seized his hair in her hands as she cried out and liquid rolled freely down across his face.

Silas tasted her juices, and with a thirst that he had never known, he lapped her up.

She shuddered over and over against him and he could feel the heat burgeoning once more in his flesh. Her juices fed his warmth until he felt that he would burst in flames, white hot, like molten iron in a smith's furnace.

But the strength she had given him held and instead of burning up in desire and lust, Silas lived on as the woman of gold slipped away from him to lie upon her back. Her breathing came in deep, full respirations. The breaths of one sated.

Her melodious voice broke the quiet as she said, "My little man…we shall amuse ourselves greatly. Again and again."

Silas thought once more that it was not a matter of choice. In that, he had no say. On the other hand, he thought that there were worse situations in which he could have found himself.

"Now," she continued, "Tell me about the human female…"

He watched the woman striding down the road. She moved quickly, her steps broad and full of purpose. Her hood was drawn over her head despite the warm weather.

The tree swayed under him, a gentle breeze shifting its great limbs. He imagined that it rocked him as a mother might with the warmth of the sunlight sifting through the leaves. From his position, high among the branches of the great oak, he could see for leagues in the distance, right to where the horizon cut away the dirt road, a dusty brown track that dwindled to a fine line before disappearing entirely.

He clambered down to the ground, licking his lips. A woman alone meant good things to Gaspard of the Green. She meant easy pickings, and that was welcome since these past few weeks travelers had been scarce and the few that he had spied upon the north to south road had been too numerous or too heavily armed for him to risk.

A lone woman, though. She would do for him just fine.

He slipped along a well-worn path, one that led from the foot of the tree to a thicket behind which he would not be seen from the road. From there, he stepped out upon a bend and a rise, carefully chosen for the fact that anyone on the road, especially those on foot, would not see the young man standing there with his sword drawn until it was too late.

Gaspard shifted and shook his arms out, trying to loosen the stiffness that came after spying from his perch overlong. He was not afraid of a sole woman traveling upon the road. However, he had learned that working alone remained difficult. Several months before, he had been part of a larger troop of highwaymen many leagues to the north. As part of the band, his confidence knew no bounds until, finally, the cruel, merciless slaughter of those who resisted their plight of being robbed had left him cold.

Here, he could do what he had to do on his own terms, without needless murder, even if it meant that the risks he took were greater on his own.

He might steal to live, but he was no murderer.

Several minutes passed before she strode into view. Instead of coming to a surprised halt at the sight of the haggard young man, sword bared upon the road before her, the woman continued her steady march, never breaking her stride until she stood just before Gaspard.

That's odd, he thought. Folk never did that. As they come over the rise, travelers one and all come to an abrupt halt, no doubt to study the young man before them and the resolve of his drawn sword.

Gaspard did not disappoint, as desperation could teach any man the grim truth of doing what was required to live. His resolve to take from others was unbending.

The woman stopped then, three steps away from Gaspard. She reached up to lift the hood away from her head and it was Gaspard who took a step backward without realizing it.

She was not a tall woman. Nor was she proportioned in the thin, willowy way of the noble women that Gaspard had chanced to see upon the road. Rather, she was robust in form, her chest full and proud with a waist that narrowed well before opening out again to inviting hips. He was sure that her *derrière* would turn the head of any man as she passed, with her wearing pantaloons in the style of men.

Her dark eyes held him, their depths an enigma, and Gaspard shook himself before lifting his sword back up in what he hoped was a menacing gesture.

"Are you a robber?" she asked. Her voice was clear and he caught himself wondering what it would be like to hear her whisper with the first light of morning dancing upon her lovely lips.

"I am," he said, "Now don't be foolish, m'lady, and pass over your coin and jewelry. Food too, if you have any. Water you can keep as the road is long until the next village."

He said the same words each time, with little variation. Travelers understood quickly that he would have his way with them, but that he meant them no real harm.

The woman before him made no move, only studying him calmly, as if he posed no threat. It was more as though she regarded him as a curiosity, a moment's diversion upon the dusty road.

She shook her head, long black hair shifting about as she did, then said, "You don't speak like a highwayman. I mean, not the way I would have imagined. Are you sure you really are one? Because if you have a doubt, I'd prefer that you let me pass by."

Her eyes were so serious that Gaspard took a moment before he realized that she was teasing him. Despite his drawn sword and desperate appearance, she was not the least bit intimidated. That would not do.

He lifted his sword and then lunged at the woman. It was a risky move, but he had practiced it well and often. She was not the first stubborn traveler he had encountered upon the road.

Instead of flinching as the sword whistled past her ear to punch a hole in folds of the woman's undone hood, she was as still as stone.

Gaspard intoned his next words, these also well practiced as he withdrew his sword just as quickly as it had come.

"I am not to be trifled with, m'lady. The next touch of my blade will see you run through and I'll have what's coming to me in the end."

She simply smiled, and Gaspard thought he heard the brittle sound of his heart breaking as that smile opened the woman's face like a flower bursting into bloom.

"Be that as it may, but I am afraid that I shall disappoint you. I have nothing of value, other than the very clothes I wear. These same were taken from behind a farmhouse where they'd been hung to dry. I am sorry, but my circumstances are just as poor as your own and I can only rest here a moment for I believe that I am being followed."

She turned away and walked to the side of the road. There was a patch of shade where she sat down without looking up at him, as if he no longer mattered.

Gaspard stood still a moment before he realized that he still brandished his sword, only now at no one. He sheathed it, feeling foolish, before joining the woman at the roadside.

"Are you thirsty?" he asked. "I've no wine, but water might do much for a parched throat."

As she had walked away from him, Gaspard had not missed the fact that she carried nothing upon her person. Nor had he missed the fact that he had not been mistaken about her *derrière*.

She replied, "Some water would be nice. Thank you."

Gaspard unslung a bladder full of fresh spring water. A lively stream ran not far from his oak tree and he had found its water clean and clear.

She took it from him and had a long swallow, wiping her chin with the back of her sleeve.

Not a noble, then, he thought. He had hoped that she would turn out to be a rich woman who had slipped away from her rich husband, off in search of a dalliance or to pretend that her life was her own for a while among the commoners.

No, she is common…maybe more so, even, than me, he thought again. Small gestures like wiping one's mouth said more than anything that passed by men's and women's lips in the guise of truth.

She gave him back the skin of water and he slung it over a shoulder. Tilting his sword up in its hilt at a sharp angle, Gaspard sat down upon the ground beside the woman and together they stared at nothing upon the dusty road before them.

"Aren't you going to ask me why I am traveling alone, or where I'm from, or anything at all?" she said at last. There was no exasperation in her voice. Rather, all he heard was a simple question, one of curiosity and nothing more. That she was so unguarded was surprising. From where he came from, there were no such things as idle remarks or careless questions.

"Only if you prefer that I do. So, why are traveling alone and where are you from? And do include anything else you have a mind to tell me." He could not help smiling as he said it.

She did not answer for a time. And when it seemed that she might not at all, she spoke.

"I've been traveling for a long while now. When I began, I walked flaming corridors of gold. But then something happened at a farm. It was an accident, but I killed someone, I think. And those burnt passages have been closed to me since.

"Perhaps it is because I claimed it for my own and it has changed, becoming something less but also something more. I don't know. Only that I had no choice. It was either that or let it eat me."

The words tumbled from her lips like the water running in the little brook in the forest. Gaspard decided that as comely as she was, she was quite mad and that explained a great deal about her comportment thus far.

Then the mention of her having killed someone and that she was being followed struck home.

Messengers had come on horseback from the north and rumor flew in all directions that a lordling's son had been murdered by a servant woman. Word was she had fled and that a handsome reward awaited whomever chanced upon her and brought her back to face justice.

Gaspard had heard the story with little interest. It had been such a short time and those messengers had been on fleet horses. A servant woman traveling on foot would take weeks, months even, to arrive this far south if south was indeed the direction she had taken.

Except that maybe she had managed it anyway.

Gaspard felt his stomach flutter with excitement. A reward would do for him what hundreds of travelers with their few coins of bent copper would never do. He could leave off with this life of misery and desperation. He might even return home triumphant before his elder brother and purchase some neighboring land to begin a proper farm alongside that of the ancestral tracts. There was never enough money for the families of the region to be able to offer all of their sons the inheritance of lands. Instead, they went to the eldest son and as for the siblings, it fell to them to strike out upon the open road, vagabonding until destiny or doom spirited them away.

But with this woman and the money she represented, Gaspard of the Green could go back to being Gaspard du Vallon, the younger son returned to the family fold, his pockets full and his future bright.

The woman beside him had fallen silent and Gaspard eased himself to his feet once more. He looked down upon the small form seated upon the ground and wondered how she might have been driven to murder a nobleman.

"When you say that you may have killed someone at a farm, you meant to say a nobleman's farm?" he asked, his hand drifting to the pommel of his sword. The movement could be construed as habit or threat. He did not care one way or the other.

She looked up at him with a puzzled face.

"No, not noble. It was a farm like any other along the road. Modest with a modest young man that was kind to me, until…" she trailed off.

Gaspard had heard the nobleman's family name with disinterest and now it escaped him. He thought it of only a syllable or two.

"I see," said Gaspard, "So this modest family, what was their name? Perron...Paran, something like that?"

"Perene?" she exclaimed. "Someone has been killed at House Perene?"

Perene...*that* was the name the horseman had mentioned. She was the one.

"Who?" she asked as she climbed to her feet, her voice filled with alarm, "Who was it?"

Gaspard replied, "Who was killed, or who did the killing, my pretty?"

He did not wait for her to answer as he tightened his grip upon his sword. He doubted she would be much trouble. She was certainly unbalanced, but she was also weaponless.

"The defunct was the nobleman's son. I don't recall his first name. As to who did for him, they say it was a servant woman who then ran off in the night, the man's blood not yet dry upon her hands."

He watched as understanding flooded her features. Emotion swirled behind her eyes as they shifted from his face to look down at his sword hand and back up at him.

"I am sorry. But you see, there is a reward," he said.

"But I know nothing of this," she said. "I left the manor during the night and I did not return. Master Olivier was alive when last I saw him."

She did not add that when she last saw him, it was with the imprint of her hand emblazoned in red upon his cheek. He had hurt her and her hand had flown of its own volition to strike the groping fool.

"Of course he was," said Gaspard, "But there are people who want to speak with you about it. We shall go together, you and I. I will be your protector and escort along the way."

Her eyes shifted again to his sword hand, then she said, "Please, don't do this. You'll regret it, I promise you, and so will I."

Gaspard did not doubt that she regretted much, but he would soon be a rich man and for that he was prepared to do what was required.

She shifted her feet and then looked up at the sun. There were no clouds to block its bright face and Gaspard watched, surprised, as she looked directly at it, wide-eyed and not forced to tighten her eyes closed under its brightness.

He slid his sword out of its sheath silently in a fluid, practiced motion. The day was beginning to warm and he wanted to be off before the heat became oppressive.

That she could look at the full sun without squinting was an interesting enough trick, but she would need to do a great deal more than that to turn him from his purpose.

She looked at him and she smiled.

He wiped at his brow with his free hand and his sleeve came away wet with perspiration. The day was warming faster than he had anticipated.

"If nothing I can say will change your mind," she said, "Then I will go with you, although the way back north is long and difficult."

He replied, "We shall continue south, in fact. There is a small city in the foothills leading up to the Ardoise mountains. It is named Licharre and there is headquartered a royally mandated prefecture. They will see you on your way to whatever end awaits you.

"Otherwise, as you say, the way to the north is long and worse than difficult," he continued, wiping again at his face. Sweat was running down to darken his shirt collar. Her eyes met his and he remarked that what he first took as mere prettiness was, in fact, a visage of remarkable beauty.

"I don't know how you managed to get past them, little woman that you are, but there is a band of brigands who control a ford along the north road and they are merciless to those who seek passage.

"To avoid them, we would need to turn far from our way to the west before continuing north, and that would be costly in time. Too much so, and they are not the only lot of villains we might encounter. As it is, I can't imagine how you managed to slip by them, as the ford is the only way you could have gotten so far south this quickly."

He knew the ford well enough. There he had seen far too many men and women slain when they posed the least resistance to being robbed. He had been there and had held a drawn bow with the rest of them as travelers were obliged to turn over their purses. Sometimes they still paid with their lives. That his own arrows always flew wide of their targets had not escaped notice and Gaspard had slipped away one night, running for all his worth to the south, always to the south.

He grimaced at the heat assailing him before shifting the sword from one hand to the other as he removed his leather vest. The linen shirt he wore underneath was drenched down his back.

"Then to the south we shall go," she said, her smile at once sad and unwavering.

"But I think you should know that your protection is not needed. You still haven't really understood who I am…what I am."

He did not follow her. It was only more of her cryptic talk, the madness that slipped through her cracked mind to confound her tongue.

What he did follow with his eyes was the line of her jaw and the way it led inevitably to her lips. He could imagine the soft skin underneath his fingertip as he traced along her face to touch those full lips.

The heat was becoming ever more intense but he barely noticed, suddenly preoccupied by the growing weight between his legs. There, a different kind of heat was burgeoning as his eyes drifted down to her chest, the gentle curves of her breasts causing her shirt to billow out in just the right way. They were full and well-formed. He could not break away, even if he knew that he should not stare. Her nipples rose up to tighten against the rough fabric of her shirt and he shifted his hips as his member thickened and lifted.

Without noticing, Gaspard let his sword fall to the ground. He stepped toward the woman before him and was gratified to see that she made no move to flee.

He looked to her eyes as his breathing deepened and for the smallest of moments, he thought he saw red flames crackling in their dark depths. He knew it was only a trick of the sunlight, nothing more, but for just an instant, it had been like looking into a smithy's forge, at blood red embers capable of melting the hardest steel.

All thought of rewards and riches drifted away. He wanted only to know the feel of her soft lips. He wanted to learn the taste of her taut nipples in his mouth. She was a thing of exquisite beauty and he had been a fool not to have seen it earlier.

"You see, I am not without defense," she said to him, her smile still there, shaped by luscious red lips that begged to be kissed.

Gaspard fell to his knees and said, "I…I was blind. I am sorry, m'lady. Please. I am clean and healthy despite my threadbare clothing."

He did not know why he said such things. Except that he now understood that she had been a goddess hiding behind the eyes of a servant woman and that he would worship at her feet, if only she would let him.

"Clean and healthy?" she said. "Then I think you must show me."

Gaspard leapt to his feet, the sweat pouring from him now, and stripped away his thin shirt before hurriedly unbuttoning his pants and kicking off his boots.

He stood before her, his body shining in the bright sunlight. He was lean with rope-like muscles. The past months on his own had stripped away what little fat he had had under his skin, leaving him hard and corded.

The dark haired woman eyed him up and down. She licked her lips and the sight of her tongue slipping out, wet and pink, only to hide itself away again just as quickly nearly made Gaspard moan.

His penis stood up stiff like a banner-man's standard. Whatever embarrassment he might have otherwise felt was gone. He only hoped that she would find him worthy.

She walked around him and with a thrill, he felt the touch of her fingertips brush across the top of his buttocks. He was burning for her and the surprise of her touch stung like hoarfrost. He shivered and his skin prickled with goosebumps.

Her dark hair tumbled around her face as she stepped around to face him once more. Her hands drifted up to tug at the laces that wound their way up the center of her shirt and Gaspard could not tear his eyes away.

She undid the laces and with an excruciating languor, she pulled open the front, letting her dark nipples, rigid and hard, slip into view.

Gaspard watched, not daring to breathe, as she unbelted her men's trousers then shrugged them away.

She pulled the shirt over her head and then stood before him, naked in the bright sun.

He saw only perfection in her every curve and as she moved away to the side of the road, he was drawn after her, as if she had bound him to her with chains.

She turned back to him and said, "Now. I want your mouth here."

She held her breasts in her hands, her nipples beckoning, and Gaspard nearly leapt at her before taking a nipple between his lips.

He ran his tongue hungrily around it, circling and revolving. His hands were around both of her breasts and they were firm and swollen in his grasp. While he tenderly mouthed one, he took the other in his fingers to roll and pull at the dark flesh that stiffened at his touch.

The sound of her voice was in his ears. Not with words but with moans of pleasure that curled around him like warm velour. The heat was becoming unbearable, but he did not care. The sun could have come down from the sky to incinerate him where he stood and it would not have mattered as long as he could die with the taste of this woman still upon his lips.

He trailed his other hand down across her flat belly to linger briefly at her navel. Then, emboldened with the lust boiling in his veins, Gaspard ran his hand farther down to where lush, velvety hair slipped between his fingers.

She was all softness and damp heat that gave way to dripping folds as he slipped his fingers inside her.

She bucked against his hand, pushing hard against his palm. Gaspard fluttered his tongue at her aureola and he held his thumb against the hardened nub at the apex of her cleft.

"What is your name?" he gasped around the nipple in his lips.

"Melisse…my name is Melisse," she replied, moaning her words more than speaking them.

"Melisse," he repeated, "My goddess, my mistress, Melisse, I am yours to command, yours to enslave. I burn for you, Melisse."

She flinched at his words, as if they conjured up a dark memory, but desire brought her back to him. Gaspard pulled at her nipple with his lips and then took it between his teeth.

Melisse moaned again and then said, "Not so long ago, you would not have even noticed me. No one ever did…not even me. And now, I need you inside me, thief."

Gaspard grinned without understanding her words as she lay down upon the fern covered ground. He dropped down between the thighs she held wide for him and without hesitation he pushed himself into her humid depths.

It was like fire that burned him with pain and pleasure mingled. Gaspard stroked in as deeply as he could while she arched her back under him. Her breasts rolled slightly to the sides in a slow, delicious motion. He could see her ribs standing out at the cusp between them and where her flat stomach began.

She moved with him, her hips matching his rhythm, the two of them thrusting against one another. Gaspard drove in deep and as he plunged, he ground his pelvis in tight against that of Melisse. She wrapped her legs around him, seizing him in an embrace of long muscles and blazing desire.

He was burning. His vision was flaring with the flames of red lust and he thrust again and again into her. She rocked against him, her breath coming quicker and quicker until he felt himself lifting up, growing rigid as his buttocks squeezed tightly. He managed another thrust before the sound of his own voice was in his ears as he orgasmed in great pumping bursts.

He hardly remarked that the sound was of screams or that his vision had been covered in darkness. His cock was twitching in endless convulsions as he heaved and thrust against the body of a goddess that he could no longer see.

The heat was blazing all around him. His head ached with it and the smell of burnt flesh was in the air.

She screamed one short strangled cry before pushing him back and away from her.

It was as though he had been released from an enormous gloved hand that blazed with all the force of a desert sun. Cool air drifted around him while the odor of cooked meat still filled his aching head. He could see nothing.

Melisse saw the thin, if well muscled, man on his knees before her. Where his eyes had been there were now two blackened pits from which smoke wisped upward as he groped blindly about.

She got to her feet, shaking, tears streaming down her face as she said, "I am sorry. I wanted only a moment with you. I have mastered the flame within me, but it remains willful and savage. You should not have tried to force me to go with you. You left me no choice."

Gaspard heard the sadness in her trembling voice and replied, "It is nothing, mistress. I have the sight of you still in my mind and if that is the last thing I shall ever see, I do not regret it."

She watched in horror as he searched about him, naked and crawling across the road, his arms outstretched.

His skin was sloughing away from him in places, most of him a sickening red in color, as if he had been boiled alive.

By chance, his hand came across the sword he had abandoned earlier in the dust. He seized it and got to his feet before saying, "I shall guard the road, Melisse, while you go on. Whoever dares follow you shall meet me and my sword and I shall strike them down."

She could see the muscles of his back twisting with his determination, the skin mostly gone as he turned unsteadily, the sword held before him, weaving weakly in the air.

"Oh, what have I done?" she said, before donning her stolen clothing.

The sense of being followed had been gaining in strength the last few days, pushing her to move ever faster. She no longer felt the need to sleep, so she had walked day and night, never stopping, for what felt like weeks gone by. But the time lost here would be difficult to catch up and she knew that each moment of not moving meant a moment closer to what felt like certain doom.

She could do nothing for him, except to cry tears of chagrin and regret.

"I am sorry," she repeated as she turned away from the burned figure upon the road, his sword still in hand.

With grim determination, she strode away and did not permit herself to look back.

Gaspard du Vallon, errant son turned highwayman and back again, held his sword tightly despite his grip being so inexplicably slippery. All was darkness and, after a time, all became silent around him. He could still hear her voice though, even when he was no longer sure that he still held his sword, or whether he still stood upon the dirt road.

He would guard her, his beautiful goddess, his mistress, the one who had blessed him between her divine thighs.

The trees swayed gently with the breeze of a beautiful day and birds began to sing songs of a joyful spring. All was calm once more as the first flies began to alight upon the body lying facedown on the road, a bloody sword still held in its charred hands.

The Marechal de Barristide looked about him.

The demon Blue had been at his side just a moment before and now, with no warning, the damnable beast had disappeared.

They had made a swift descent from the witch's swamp toward the south and the Marechal grudgingly had to admit that the demon never slowed him.

The thing moved with frightening speed and silence yet seemed to take no interest in the Marechal whatsoever. Even if, once or twice, he thought he saw the six-legged creature eyeing his horse, its slick blue tongue slipping out from between hundreds of needle-like teeth.

As for being an excellent tracker as promised by the witch, the Marechal's opinion was more reserved. The demon never seemed to take an interest in the direction they chose as they traveled these many days southward and it was only now, before a river crossing, that it had done anything at all remarkable. That it chose this moment to desert seemed more than suspect to the Marechal.

His horse picked her way gingerly down the slope to the river rushing before them. The Marechal feared that he might go many leagues downstream in search of a narrows shallow enough to ford. To his relief, he saw a cabled ferry meant for carrying both man and beast across the frothing torrent.

With a heavy thud, an arrow sprouted in a wooden post of the ferry's framework and a deep voice rang out.

"Ho, there! Yer'll stay where ye be and make no move for that pretty cutter at yer side. Me men have ye surrounded and the next *fléche* will find itself growing out yer gorry throat and not some poor old post."

The Marechal held still. He had no fear of arrows, not for him. But he would risk no harm to his horse and an arrow could fly astray far too easily.

He would wait until they closed in.

With dry forest leaves crunching underfoot, he heard them come and he sighed. He had hoped that as with most brigands upon the provincial roads they would be few, most of the time numbering less than ten. But the footsteps he heard from all around him told a different story. There were certainly at least twenty men encircling him, and his odds at making a clean escape had just taken a turn for the worse.

"Might I dismount, at the least?" the Marechal shouted out. "Should a nervous finger loose an errant shot, I'd prefer that my horse not take injury."

There was no answer, so he slowly lifted one leg free of its stirrup and dropped to the ground. He backed away from his mare and then turned to face the surrounding trees.

Dark, grimy faces peered back at him. Their eyes seemed overly white and he understood that they had darkened their features as a means of camouflage.

There were just three of them within view but among the brush surrounding the clearing, the Marechal could make out branches that shook unnaturally. There was the ever present sound of dry leaves crackling under the feet of men who moved with caution to keep their bows trained upon their target.

One of the men in front of him, a notched and rusted sword in hand where the other two held drawn short bows, stepped forward and said, "Me scouts sawn a great dog at yer side, some leagues back." The Marechal recognized the voice from earlier.

"Where'in he be now, yer puppy?" he asked.

"He's not mine," replied the Marechal. "And he comes and goes as he pleases."

The swordsman was a hulking figure, but he stood back and said, "Garn. And yer've a fair size to ye. 'Carry ye a purse just as big, mebbe?"

The Marechal held his hands loosely at his sides, keeping himself relaxed despite the frenetic energy boiling just under the surface of his calm demeanor.

Blood would spill, and sooner rather than later, he knew, no matter how much coin he carried.

"I have gold and silver," he said, "I'll give it over without resisting. In exchange, let me leave here with my horse and I'll go back the way I came."

The man tipped his sword down, letting the tip sink into the dirt at his feet and laughed.

"Let 'im leave? Whaddya'all think m'boys?" he said, raising his voice.

"Me, I'm a'thinkin that we'll takes yer gold and silver, and then we'll lay hands on that pretty pony, too. Ye seems s'worried about 'er, I'm guessin' she's worth more than yer purse of coin."

The Marechal sighed and rolled his shoulders slowly. He felt sure that he could drop to the ground and roll while drawing his sword. That would foul the feet of the two bowmen, standing too closely together as they were, and with some luck, arrows would fly and hamper or even kill the one with the rusted sword. If not, it would not be the first time that the Marechal was obliged to fight with his back upon cold ground and he knew his chances were good that if it went well, the men hiding among the trees would slink away rather than risk up close fighting.

Or the next moment might find him a walking pincushion.

His hand flexed as he readied himself to drop. The swordsman's eyes narrowed but in the next half breath, a blood-curdling scream from within the trees broke the silence, only to be cut off clean.

The bowmen wavered, turning to look over their shoulders. From the opposite side of the clearing, another scream erupted to be choked off just like the first.

The swordsman's eyes flew wide and he hissed, "Ye voyage alone, or no?"

The Marechal simply shrugged just as another man let out a yelping cry not far away.

The two bowmen looked to their chief, eyes even whiter than before. And then, without a word, they loosened their hold upon their bowstrings and strode off into the woods, looking wildly about.

A moment later, there were choked screams and bushes shaking from all around the clearing.

The Marechal gave the swordsman a smile as he slid his shining blade from its scabbard.

"I travel alone. At least, that is, if we don't count the *dog*," he said.

The bandit threw his sword up in front of him as the Marechal advanced, ready to send a flurry of thrusts and parries destined only to confuse the man before he would close and open the dirty fool's throat with the *main-gauche* sheathed and waiting upon his opposite thigh.

But before the Marechal could do more than ready himself, the brigand raised his blade and then it was as though an invisible hook had sunk into the man's spine before he was jerked backward, folding over nearly in two as his feet flew off the ground.

Out of sight, another horrified scream erupted before coming to a sudden end and all fell to an eerie silence.

The Marechal stood his ground, turning slowly upon his heel. He expected an arrow to come whistling out from the trees or, perhaps, that several men might try to rush him in a last desperate attempt.

Instead, there was nothing.

He listened and, finally, he went back to his horse standing calmly as she always did while waiting for him.

The Marechal patiently coaxed her onto the flat wooden ferry and then seized the rope threaded through great black iron eyelets sunk into the ferry's side.

It was a job meant for several men, as the river's current was strong. The Marechal pulled, his broad chest straining at the seams of his fine white shirt, and although it was slow going, he eventually made headway and came to land upon the opposite side of the torrent.

Astride his mount once more, they climbed up the embankment and took up the road that led south.

After less than a league, he rounded a bend and the mare snorted, nearly rearing into the air. Only one thing made her otherwise calm demeanor turn so skittish, and that was the six-legged beast conjured by a swamp witch.

Blue stood before them, its wide mouth stretched in a tooth-laden grin. The Marechal started as he saw what looked like the outline of a man's foot pushing out from the skin of the creature's belly. A belly now overstretched to what should have been the bursting point, with whatever that was inside not quite dead.

The fine silver chain that wrapped about the demon's chest and torso had shifted and loosened. As the beast moved toward him, the Marechal remarked that its normally silent glide had given way to a ponderous waddle and a strange slithery sound.

Its six legs were too short, it seemed, and as Blue came up alongside him, the Marechal saw that its distended belly dragged upon the ground.

"All of them?" he asked, not expecting an answer.

"Well, it will serve you right if you have indigestion, you foolish beast. No good ever comes of gluttony."

The Marechal nudged the mare with his heels and they set off, the Ardoise mountain range with its snow-covered peaks to the south now plainly in view.

Mesrin bent down and slipped his hand inside the still-warm flesh while he said, "Wisp, I think things might have taken an unforeseen turn, after all."

The thin woman standing beside the bent over form said nothing, a frown upon her lips and her brow furrowed deeply.

"My flame should have woken to mischief by now before incinerating that stupid bitch. I was expecting to gather it back to me, but there is no sign of it."

He lowered and twisted his arms, straining as he worked.

"What does that mean for us?" the woman said at last. Her skin glowed gently despite the afternoon sun blazing down upon them.

"It means that there will be some consternation among those who worry about such things. My sister, for example, or even more likely, her mate, Raffiran. The humorless brute will not see the amusement that this might have garnered for all of us.

"No, he will be quick to action, I should think. Although he would never deign to exert himself personally in the affair."

The woman's glowing skin flared for an instant and she took a full step backward.

"Do you mean…?" her voice trailed off to a whisper that spoke of fear as she looked furtively about her.

"I suppose so, yes. The beast will have been sent, so we shall need to be quick about our business here."

He stood up, the skin of the farmer in his hands still warm. He shrugged it on and turned about as he adjusted it upon his golden form.

The openings for where the man's eyes had been were askew and as Mesrin wrenched them into place, he looked about him for the Will O' Wisp that had accompanied him thus far.

But he was alone.

He kicked the dirt at his feet, small pebbles and dust falling onto the bloody corpse lying on the ground.

"You bitch," he grated. Then, he looked quickly about him, his visage pinching with fear inside the farmer's sloppily fitted face.

He must move and be swift to find the woman he had encountered in the forest. If he could, he would recuperate his given flame and hold it in evidence that Raffiran's horrid creature should turn aside.

He raised his arms and a wind lifted in the otherwise calm afternoon as thick dust whirled around him. It quickly coalesced into a small tornado and Mesrin leapt clumsily astride the vortex, seizing threads of the turning wind in hands that slipped and shifted in his grip like poorly fitted gloves.

The farmer had been a very fat man, but Mesrin had had no time to choose better.

He lifted strands of living wind, twisted them into reins and gave them a snap. With a snarl, the whirlwind leapt forward and sped southward, the being upon its back hunched over and holding tight.

"So what can you tell me about her?" she asked as she snapped closed the second manacle around his wrist. The golden hued female had already bound him at the ankles, his legs spread wide and now both arms followed suit.

Silas frowned and said, "I would have told you about her without being chained to the floor like this."

"Oh, I believe you. It's just that Raffiran would never let me do such a thing. He is very good at what he does, but uninterested in experimentation. But to see a man left to such vulnerability…well, I find it just so enticing."

Her glowing skin shifted colors, from gold to russet orange and back again. Silas knew that she was growing excited by his present circumstances while he only felt foolish and annoyed. She had meant every word when she had described him as her new plaything and despite the reaction of his body at her touch, he found it to his dislike.

"And if I refuse to speak about her until you release me?" he asked.

Gold shifted to a red that deepened to ruddy burgundy. Silas bit his lip, wondering if he had dared too much.

"In that case, I shall ravish you and split you wide the way the men of your world cleave trees of the forest with iron axes that bite deep with each swing," she replied.

The voice that had been so musical now turned dark and menacing.

"Do not think that I cannot. Do not suppose that I am incapable of rapine and violence, that I am constrained in the way that human females are.

"I choose this form because it suits me, but I can change if I must."

And before Silas could utter a word, the female called Lest spread her legs and from between her thighs there was movement.

She shifted and her cleft opened slowly. Absurdly, Silas was reminded of a crawling snail as her clitoris lifted free from her folds, thickening and lengthening.

"I would use this to open you wide and I would teach you to never speak to me with that insolent tone again."

Silas swallowed as she advanced toward him. From between her legs had risen what was not quite a penis, but it was thick, long and pulsing with what might have passed for her heartbeat.

His own member lifted in response and he clenched his jaw tightly.

Her breasts are so round, so perfect, he reminded himself. My body answers to a woman, that is all.

Desperately, he tried to look away, to keep in mind her lovely hips, her almond shaped eyes. But he was helpless as his breathing became shallow and his tumescence ripened with each passing moment.

"I don't know who she is," he gasped, "I don't know where she came from or where she was going."

Lest said, "There. You see, little man, you can be reasonable."

She moved close to him and he looked up to see her newly formed member sliding back from view. Her blood red color calmed to her usual golden tones as she straddled his prone form.

"So, instead of telling me what you don't know, why not begin with what you do?"

She lowered herself down upon him, her crotch forcing his cock down against his stomach without taking him inside her. He groaned with the pleasure and pain of her weight pinning him that way.

"Her eyes," he began, "They were dark as she passed me in the night."

Lest moved slowly, sliding her crotch forward and then drifting slowly back. Silas could feel her wetness engulfing him.

"But as she tried to sneak by me, I saw the color of the moon gleaming in her eyes. They shined with the gold of moonset in autumn and she moved in silence.

"I would have sworn that she was a ghost and when I looked again to the sky, I saw heavy clouds blanketing the moon. I knew that whatever was reflected in her eyes came from within and not the heavens."

Lest flexed her hips again, sliding along his length until she arrived at the tip where she hesitated, her lips coming to rest positioned around but not over his head.

Silas groaned and tried to push himself up and inside her, but his metal bindings held him fast where he was.

"I waited," he gasped, "I wasn't sure of what I had seen. My curiosity got the better of me though, so I went quietly to our barn which was the only place she could have gone.

"I found her sleeping in the hayloft, hiding down inside the straw except for one of her feet sticking up, and when she came out her eyes weren't filled with moonlight but with simple loneliness instead."

The golden woman moved her hips in very small, very slow circles, Silas' cock never quite entering her.

Her breasts mirrored her movements in a pendulous way that mesmerized him.

"But there was bravery, too…such courage there that it drew me to her like a lodestone. And she made me laugh despite myself."

Lest leaned over to let her breasts drop down, her nipples drifting across Silas' chest. The touch was like that of soft down and with a sigh, she engulfed him, taking him deep inside her as she slid back to ride upon his hips.

"What you say and what you mean are two different things, aren't they?" she asked as she rode up and down upon his shaft.

"I don't understand," he replied, groaning.

"There is more than admiration in your words," she said.

Silas replied, "She was the first woman I had ever known."

"Well, it is true that one never forgets their first time, but as your second, perhaps I am not so bad."

She increased her rhythm then, inciting Silas to move against the chains that bound him. He did what he could to move with her until they had both closed their eyes, their breathing quick and shallow.

With a cry, Silas came hard, pumping into her, but what he saw in his mind's eye was the dark haired woman in the barn. He came with heavy spasms of his abdomen, seeing only her with straw in her hair and those dark eyes that held him and only him for a time.

Lest stood up suddenly then and looking down upon him, she said, "You laughed just now. It was a sound that came from deep within your heart."

She took a step backward, frowning.

"It was not for joy of me, was it?"

She did not wait for an answer and left him there, shackled to the floor.

Silas turned his head away. His only thought, in bitterness, was that he did not even know the mysterious woman's name.

My moon girl, he thought. I shall call you that until the day I find you and ask what else I might call you.

They moved more slowly now that Blue was so encumbered.

The road they followed snaked its way through thickets that opened into farmer's fields stretching to the far horizons lying to the east and west. But ever present to the south loomed the Ardoise mountains with their white peaks of eternal snow.

The Marechal had heard of them, but only in reference to the quality of the stone work used to cover homes with roofs that, if well done, never leaked in contrast to the baked earthen tiles that were slowly replacing them.

It was from these mountain flanks that roofing slate was struck, but the mountains were just as well known for their peril to those voyagers seeking passage to the southern face and the warmer climes beyond.

He rode with a measured cadence that would not tax his mount. It was one that seemed more in keeping with the demon's current bloated state.

As they rounded a turn, the travelers came to a fork. On one side, the wide road continued its meandering course to the left, while to the other side there was a narrow, meaner track that led in a direct line toward the southern mountains.

The Marechal paid little attention to what appeared to be a simple farmer's path until Blue waddled forward to nose at the path. He lifted its head up, sickly as he was, and gave a half-hearted wiggle that rolled down his bloated trunk as he looked back at the Marechal upon his horse.

The Marechal turned to watch and the demon wiggled again before walking forward upon his six legs, parting the long grasses that nearly hid the little used road as he did.

The Marechal shrugged and nudged his horse to follow the creature. The road they had been following seemed to ramble far to one side and then to the other, and as much as he could tell, the Marechal could not make out where in the countryside the road builders had been obliged to let it. There were no unsurmountable obstacles in what should have been a direct way to the south. Instead, their way had twisted and turned like a snake and continued to try the

Marechal's patience even if he was not sure that they were truly on the runaway woman's trail.

In any case, the narrow, unkempt road they were on now did not meander. Rather, it ran straight and the Marechal could not help but think it was more direct, but to what end he could not say. As for the demon, if he knew he kept it to himself.

As the sun rose to its midday peak, they came upon a small cottage alongside the road. An elderly man wearing clothing riddled with holes was in a vegetable patch, hoeing with little enthusiasm between rows of onion and garlic.

A tiny wrinkled woman popped out the front door of the house and shrieked, "Nestor!"

The old man continued hoeing and the Marechal smiled. It was only with the grace earned after many years together that old men and women could manage to so thoroughly ignore one another. The Marechal noted that the old fellow never even twitched, which made him doubt for a moment that the man was stone deaf. And on the heels of that thought was the fact that the woman would not have bothered to call him if he was.

She held up a hand to shield her eyes, staring out at the large man upon his horse.

The Marechal was not worried about the demon on the ground beside him. The witch spoke truly that people would only see a large dog if they noticed him at all. Rather, he thought the old woman was just surprised that someone had been foolish enough to have left the main road for the cowpath they were on now.

She came out of the house with creaky steps and the old man finally stopped his hoeing to cast an eye in their direction.

"Lost yer way, have ya?" he asked the Marechal.

"Could be that I have," the man upon his horse replied before slipping down from his saddle.

"Do you have water to spare for my horse and me?" the Marechal asked.

"Aye," replied the old man. The woman joined the old man at his side and squinted at the Marechal with her eyes nearly shut.

"And you don't ask for your dog, do you?" she asked. Her visage reminded the Marechal of the little dolls peasant folk make, carving faces into apples to dry and wrinkle in the sun.

"Oh…well, the dog doesn't belong to me, you see. As it is, he fends for himself."

The old man dropped his gaze to the demon, saying, "Looks green around the gills if ya ask me."

Startled, the Marechal looked sharply down at the beast. He had never noticed gills on the demon before. Instead of gills, though, he only saw a ridiculously swollen demon with a head hanging low and no sign of his habitual toothy smile

"He means," the old woman said, "that the dog which doesn't belong to you looks sick."

The Marechal sighed with relief. "Ah, it might be something he ate."

The old man lifted his hoe to point to the side of the modest house and there the Marechal saw a roofed water well.

He led his horse over and worked on raising water one bucket at a time to fill a large trough just beside the well.

"So, yer lost then?" The old man had wandered over, leaving his hoe and the woman behind.

The Marechal replied, "That remains to be seen. Can you tell me if there is a city lying to the south, before one comes to the mountains themselves?"

"Aye, there be a *ville* named Licharre in the foothills. Of fair size, 'tis, with commodities of every sort. And if yer lookin' for passage over the mountains, then it's the only way ya can go.

"If that's where yer headed, turns out that yer not so lost as ya think."

"And why is that?" asked the Marechal.

"The road ya left to take this 'un runs every which way but straight. It promenades travelers through every piss pot village along the way and as it happens, there's inns in those villages, built special for travelers, and them's inns are each one owned by the same fellows who had the road built."

"I see," said the Marechal before dipping his entire head into the trough.

He came up sputtering and raked his thick hair back from his face.

"If the *ville*'s where ya want to go," continued the old man, "Then this old road is the one that'll get ya there quickest. 'Twas a time that this was the only road, afore those money grubbers came up with a way to milk folk dry long before they ever get there."

The two men came back to the road and the old woman who continued to stare down at the demon.

The Marechal saw that Blue had more than lost his grin. His face had taken a decidedly downward turn and his throat appeared to be in spasms.

With a terrible sound, the demon lurched backward while opening its gullet wide and there, before the three of them, he coughed up a slimy mess.

It was a man's boot, covered in viscous fluids. The stench of it was like that of a corpse.

The demon backed away, shaking its head from side to side before suddenly freezing, rigid and quivering. He craned his head slowly upward, and if he had had ears, the Marechal could have imagined them swiveling in every direction as the demon seemed to hear something.

The old man chose that moment to say, "I don't think ya should feed your dog boots anymore."

"He's not my dog," replied the Marechal distractedly as he watched the demon. The infernal smile was back and the scarred man could not help but notice the leather boot laces dangling from between its teeth.

The demon looked directly into the Marechal's eyes and wriggled his body before turning to stare down the road to the south, then bringing his gaze back to the Marechal.

The Marechal turned to the old couple, saying, "It seems that we shall be leaving. But before we do, I wonder if you might have something other than water to drink. I have coin to pay for it."

The old woman shook her head.

"You'll not find anything stronger than well water here, I'm afraid." She looked beyond the Marechal and with a start, said, "Looks like your dog run off."

"Capucine, the man says the dog h'aint his," the old man said, exasperated.

The Marechal turned about, looking for where the beast might have gone. But there was no sign of the thing.

Shrugging, he asked the old man, "In your estimation, is the nearest wine in a southerly direction, or is it back trail on the other road at one of those inns you mentioned?"

"That's a clear'un. Ya just keep a'goin the way yer've been. This old road'll have ya at the *ville* with a few days to spare and that'll be in the bottom side o'town where drink and shelter h'aint so pricey.

"Used to be the quarter of abattoirs and leather makers. Nowadays, it's mostly whores and their ilk, but the wine flows well enough and won't burn too many holes in yer wallet or yer gullet."

The Marechal nodded and climbed back upon his horse.

"Say," the old man continued, "Did ya come across a band of nasties up north there? Near the river fording?"

The Marechal grinned and said, "I don't believe you need worry about that bunch anymore. It seems that something swallowed them up."

He gave the reins in his hands a gentle shake. The mare, her thirst assuaged, broke into a light trot that would carry them steadily toward the gleaming mountain peaks and cheap whore's wine.

"Say there, Capucine. Did'ya mark the scar a'running down that cavalier's face?" the old man asked, watching the man upon his horse shrink in the distance.

The old woman frowned, her eyes crinkling like parchment paper as she did.

"Yes, I did. Now stop that ridiculous accent, Nestor. You sound like a fool."

The old man only grunted, and if he did it with an accent, she could not tell.

"And get that boot underground, back behind the cabbages before it starts to stink even worse."

The old man sighed and said, "And why ever would it stink worse than it already does, dear wife?"

"Piss in my pocket, you old fool," she swore, "There happens to be a foot still inside it."

The old man nodded and replied, "That was no dog, was it?"

"No, dear husband, dogs don't walk on six legs and eat men whole. Now get to burying that mess and come inside quick after.

"It's one thing to keep us hidden from brigands with simple cantrips, but it is well beyond my power to withstand whatever doom follows in that scarred man's wake."

Nestor nodded and moved as quickly as his old bones would let him as he went in search of a shovel. At the least, there would be no more hoeing between rows that day, which was something, after all.

The city, or *ville* as the old man called it, of Licharre started modestly enough.

The Marechal found himself almost from one moment to the next riding between simple homes that were built closer and closer together as he rode, until the streets narrowed abruptly into what amounted to cobbled pedestrian passages with buildings springing up to overhang the street.

The sunlight could not filter directly down as it had in the countryside and the Marechal was soon in passages that dimmed long before the setting sun rode round the world, giving way to the Moon's rule and her courtesan, Night, for a time.

He dismounted and took his mount's reins in hand. Better that he walk and have his eyes on the folk he passed. If anyone made a move, at ground level he would be better able to deal with it.

He felt that his chances were good that the servant woman, Melisse, would be obliged to pass through Licharre.

If her goal was to flee ever southward and beyond the mountains, then the city would surely draw her in and from there she would search out the common folk's quarter where she could blend in. The bourgeois of the city were the same kind of people that she had left behind in Perene Manor and that would not sit well with a servant.

Here, she would feel among her own. The Marechal had only to wait her out.

And, as promised by the old man on the road, he soon came upon an establishment with its wooden sign hung upon creaking, rusted chains, *La Pagaille*.

It appeared to be a sort of auberge, if not rather seamy. The low murmur of many voices coming from within spoke to the Marechal of wine and perhaps even a bed without too many fleas where he might spend the night after so many under starry skies.

A stable boy came quickly from around the corner of the building and said with a lilting, sing-song accent, "Ah'll see to yer horse, m'sieur, if ye've a mind to go inside."

The boy's words were nearly incomprehensible to the Marechal's ears, but when he worked them out, he replied, "That's fine, boy. Get her fed, watered, and rubbed down. My saddle needs oiling as well."

He fished under his belt and found a shining coin to flip into the air.

The stable boy plucked it out of the air neatly and then, seeing the size of it in his hand, he said, "But m'sieur, t'is enough to keep her stabled for six months!"

"I don't expect that I shall stay as long as that. Just the same," said the Marechal, "You'll take care that she has good oats and that the livery master examines her irons. When I'll next need to ride, I want to do so without worrying she might throw a shoe."

The boy smiled wide, saying, "Yessir, he will, and the very best grain we've got is hers," before he took the reins and led the mare away.

The Marechal went up the wooden steps leading to the interior of the auberge and let the dark air, tainted with the odors of spilled ale and too many unwashed bodies, swallow him whole.

The day's warmth did not make its way far inside, so the Marechal eased through the overcrowded tables and chairs to a corner somewhat removed from the dense center. There he found an iron grate upon bowed legs that had been recently loaded with glowing coals.

He pulled up a rickety chair to an even more rickety table and signaled to a serving girl…

✧ ✧ ✧

Capucine, an herb witch once accustomed to spending her days making healing poultices for the tired feet of pilgrims headed south over the mountains, stirred the contents of the black iron pot and poured in a handful of dust from a jar.

The water seethed for a moment, then calmed. She poked at the embers glowing beneath what some might have called a cauldron and murmured a few words she had learned at the knee of her grandmother.

The front door creaked open and closed and the floorboards followed suit as Nestor ambled into the room, wiping at his forehead with a handkerchief.

"How I hate burying anything, dear wife," he said. "It just seems so circular a thing to do with far too much perspiration involved."

"Shhhh!" hissed the old woman.

Seeing the iron pot, one that was normally stored away deep inside a back cupboard, Nestor closed his mouth around his next words.

When his wife was about her divination, he knew that it was never for want of a good reason. Portents were what called to her and when she went to the trouble of it, there were foul things afoot.

She leaned over the water, peering deeply into its surface as bits of ground leaves churned about. Nestor heard her whisper in a language that he had heard many times, but of which he understood nothing.

A sound began. The old man would have liked to say that it came from the steaming water, but for the fact that it felt as though it came from inside his own head, deep between his ears.

It grew swiftly. A keening, musical sound like that of flutes played by sainted men walking with bloody feet over hallowed ground, and in that melody there were notes that cut like knives. An infinite sadness that ebbed and flowed, speaking of death and of despair.

Capucine pulled herself back from the water, her eyes flying wide as she threw a heavy piece of cured leather over the cauldron.

The sound was muffled and as she rasped out other words, ones that made Nestor's skin jitter and his jaw clench tight as the sad melody dwindled to blessed silence.

"Capucine," he whispered, almost too afraid to cast his trembling voice into the now quiet room. "What was it, my love? What did you see?"

She turned to him and he saw that she wrung her aged hands, one within the other, over and over. Her voice shook as she said, "Husband, pray that it pass by us in its haste. Pray that it not remark two old hearts beating behind these thin walls.

"For should it not, what comes will be the end of us. Its white purity holds blades that will scythe us down like wheat, our very souls but chaff before its fury."

Nestor swallowed, unsure if his wife was still in the throes of her divination. He hoped instead, and in weak selfishness, that she was and that her words were meant for some other poor folk about to meet their doom.

"Now be still, my husband. It is not far now and moves swiftly."

He did not dare to utter another word. Instead, he walked softly to his woman and put his arms around her.

Nestor did not know why they should deserve such a fate for the simple act of assuaging a traveler's thirst. But he had lived long enough to know that life promised nothing of justice and that if he should die this day, at least it would be with his wife in his arms. Which was something, after all.

The Marechal signaled to a serving girl for another cup of wine. His table was strewn with dented pewter cups that tipped and rolled as he shifted upon an uncomfortable chair.

He had drunk deeply and did not yet consider the deed finished as he tried to wash away the dust of so many roads that clung to him like guilt. His vision remained clear though, and he scanned the dark features arrayed before him.

There were merchant men, some more successful than others with straw-wrapped carafes and grey metal cups before them. Others contented themselves with the pale yellow ale brewed on the premises, drinking it down from cracked wooden bowls.

Prostitutes meandered from one table to the next, smiling and nodding to the men working so hard to get drunk. When one chanced to catch a man's eye, she would plunk herself down beside him or even perch upon the hapless fool's knee as she did what she could to ply him with her charms.

The Marechal had waved away more than one as they worked the room. He was the newcomer and no doubt the women judged him by the quality of his clothing that there was money to be made if the man could be lured by their wiles.

For now they contented themselves with others, but their heavy eyes slipped back to the large man with the scar upon his face, patient and waiting until the wine did its work to lower his guard and loosen his pursestrings.

The Marechal was not duped, though, and resolved to drink his fill. He could not remember when last he had slipped from sobriety to inebriation, or even if he still could.

The servant girl threaded her way through the crowd, expertly dodging grimy hands reaching for a feel as she passed by, her hips swaying and the tray balanced over her head while one hand moved in gentle counterpoint.

She arrived with her mouth moving slightly and the Marechal guessed that she was tallying his cups.

"M'sieur, ye started fair enough with that shiny coin of yers, but it'll take another if ye mean to git yer head turned 'round," she said. She smiled and the Marechal noted that she still had all her teeth, that her life as a barmaid had not yet taken its toll.

"And will this do, then, for you to keep the wine flowing?" the scarred man said while holding up another shining coin, only this one glinted yellow and not the dull silver of the last.

The girl's eyes went wide and the Marechal continued, "It is more than fair, to be sure, and with it I expect a room for the night, as well. With a clean bed and as far removed from the commercial activities of this establishment as possible."

Seeing her brows wrinkle as she tried to work out what he had just said, he explained, "I mean that I want a quiet room and one that doesn't share a whore's wall."

The girl nodded and took the coin with enthusiasm from the Marechal's outstretched hand.

She set down yet another pewter cup filled near to the brim with a red wine so dark the Marechal might have thought it black and not burgundy. The flavor was rich and acidic, of Kaurish origin he guessed, aged little and meant for drinking fresh.

He found it well enough and as he took the cup into his hands, the servant girl gave him an appraising look and said, "And if m'sieur would like summ'un to warm his bed, there be t'other girls than tired out whores who'd be willin'."

He glanced up at her as she lingered next to him. She was well built and sturdy, appearing to be cleaner than most of the people in the auberge.

"What is your name?" he asked.

"Harnei, m'sieur…and if ye decides it'd be to yer likin', ye have but to ask anyone and I'll come to pass some time."

She turned briskly away, her skirts swirling as she went, and the Marechal watched, amused, as her hips swayed once more, only now her movements were exaggerated, daring the scarred man to look away.

A quick glance back over her shoulder, to reassure herself that he still watched, and then she flounced off, called to her service once more.

Perhaps a bed this night warmed by a young woman named Harnei, the Marechal mused.

If there was an advantage to sleeping under the stars, he had to admit that he noticed it less that he slept alone when rocks and stubborn tree roots did their best to rob him of a good night's sleep.

Being alone. It was what he had known for so many years now, it had become a way of life. He knew that it weighed upon him, as heavy as any of life's burdens, lost in his own solitude.

There were passing moments, burning hot and bright for the space of an hour or two, only for him to see the back of the woman as she went away as they always do. Their faces blurred in his memories, so many women known for but a few moments becoming one woman, one that remained forever a stranger and ever hastening to leave him.

And then he saw her. It was when they all did.

The door opened, letting in a faint glow of evening light, then it shut again quietly as a woman stepped into the crowded room.

She was not tall nor otherwise remarkable, but her presence engendered a wave of turning heads that washed across the room. Her chin was held high and her dark eyes smoldered with confidence as she walked past men who fell silent, forgetting the ale lifted to their lips, their eyes riveted upon the slight form as she moved with hips that rolled deliciously as she walked.

Long black hair fell past her shoulders and her skin was the pale color of cream. The Marechal and his eyes trained for details took her in as she sat down at a table opposite his own on the other side of the crowded room.

He watched as the serving girl, Harnei, went to the woman, bending low to say something. The woman shook her head slowly and the serving girl stood up straight, shrugging her shoulders before hastening to another table where empty cups were clattering to the floor.

The Marechal tried to look away, thinking that the woman was as ordinary as any other, but his gaze was drawn back to her over and over. There was something there, something about her and the supreme confidence in her gait that spoke to him.

As he watched from his dark corner, he noted her oval visage, delicate in some ways, robust in others. She was an amalgam of light and dark, colors running to shades of grey and it only served to make her more beautiful.

And that, the Marechal had to admit, was what she was. Of an extraordinary beauty that was all the more elegant because it lay barely hidden under the surface, a sense of strength clothed in just enough sadness that it rendered her exquisite.

He decided it was also because she did not know. She was unaware of the beauty that hid within her, which only led the Marechal to the mystery that was the confidence exuding from her in every gesture.

She was sure of herself in a way that he had only seen in foolish men, too confident of their brutish strength or too habituated to leadership inherited but not truly merited.

But hers was a self-assurance that did not appear unfounded, although why that might be, the Marechal could not say. Only he knew that it was the calm, steady attitude of someone who believed she held the mastery of her destiny firmly in her hands.

People around the Marechal began to stand and mill about. The auberge had become warmer, the air thickening. The scarred man glanced to the brazier not far from him, but the bright red coals there had slumped down to grey white lumps that should not have provided any heat.

Still, people fanned themselves as perspiration ran down their necks. The bosoms of women sparkled like dew as rivulets coalesced to pool between their breasts. Men licked their lips, mopping at their foreheads with handkerchiefs as they watched the whores swaying among them.

Soon there were those who shed their shirts as their sweat ran. Even the Marechal was moved to unbutton his doublet as he watched men and women move to brush against one another.

At first, it seemed to be by error or simple awkwardness, but bodies began to press tightly against one another and the Marechal heard sighs and groans punctuate the low murmur of the room.

He saw women straddling men's thighs, shifting their hips back and forth. He saw men's eyes rolling like horses gone wild, their trousers swelling at the crotch.

Then *her* eyes locked onto his own and in them he saw a flash. It could not have been recognition, because he did not know her, but the flash was there all the same and now she was the one who did not look away as she stared back at him.

With a nod, she motioned to the stairwell, there where a steady stream of whores and clients went to mount the steps leading to bedchambers never intended for sleeping.

He stood up to find the serving girl, Harnei, standing in his way. He stepped to the side and she moved with him, perspiration beading upon her face. Her lips were swollen and red, her blouson studded by two nipples surrounded by damp aureoles that rendered the fabric all but transparent.

The Marechal pushed her aside as gently as he could and heard the woman moan as she tried to cling to him. But the scarred man only had eyes for the dark-haired figure disappearing up the staircase and did not notice he was being followed.

He took the stairs two at a time despite the rising temperature of the auberge, and at the top of the staircase he saw a shadow slipping behind a door that did not quite close shut.

The Marechal followed, making a deliberate effort to calm himself, to master the fire building within him. He slowed his steps as he walked down the corridor and took deep breaths of the heavy air.

The door opened at his touch and he stepped into the dark interior. There was no light, not even a candle but he felt her there, a sexual presence that provoked him, that excited him.

There were no words and he needed no light to guide him to her as his hands found the heat of her being. He touched her upon her shoulders and then traced the outline of her body, first reaching up to a graceful neck that led to the soft skin of her face, then his hands swept down to caress her lightly ribbed sides and on to full, voluptuous hips that were meant for a man's hands to hold.

He brought his head to her neck, moving his lips ever so lightly along the path traced by his fingers just a moment before. Her skin was like silk, her scent clean and fresh, hinting of apples and lilac.

She moved under his touch and warm, wet lips found his as they embraced in the darkness. The Marechal had known many women, and most had been but fleeting experiences, but the touch of this woman twisted his guts and made his hands tremble like leaves upon a tree.

He might have believed himself a young man once more, about to make love for the first time, his body abuzz and vibrating at the least sensation. Her tongue slipped between his lips to tease and play against his own. He responded in kind, momentarily forgetting his hands, all his attention focused upon the sweet taste of her upon his lips.

Then it was she who took his strong hands in her own to guide him to her full breasts. He hefted them and ran his thumbs across large nipples that tightened into erection at his touch. With reluctance, he dropped his hands down, searching for where her chemise began so that he might free her of her clothing.

She stepped back from him and he heard faint rustling, a woman's quiet laughter, then there was soft, bare skin in his hands and he hesitated no longer.

In a single smooth motion, the Marechal dipped down to pick her up in his arms and strode upon strong legs to the bed among the shadows.

She sighed as he lay her upon the coverlet and he wasted no time in stripping his own clothing away.

The Marechal eased himself down to her and long thighs opened, welcoming him in the way given to women.

Instead, his lips found her nipples and he suckled at them as a child, feeling the body under him arching and small hands flying to his neck to cradle his head with a sigh. He slipped his head in between her breasts, searching for her scent of apples and lilac, finding only the delicate odors of a young woman and the salt of her perspiration.

She rocked her hips upward, urging him to mount her with his body, but the scarred man would not be hurried, preferring to draw the moment out before exquisite release.

He lifted himself off her body and used his tongue and his lips to map the contours of her belly. The terrain was firm yet yielding and as he flourished in concentric circles about her navel, the scent of musky arousal made his nostrils flare.

She shifted beneath him with near silent whimpers and finally, the Marechal brought himself to bear.

His hips dropped into line with hers, then he pulled back and down to find her humid depths. The head of his cock slipped gently into her folds, the thick humidity enveloping him in heat.

The Marechal held himself from plunging forward, choosing instead to draw himself back only to slip upward to caress the velvet kernel that rose to greet him. She moaned aloud then, the sound almost familiar to him, then he pulled back and with frank determination dove into her.

She clasped him to her body in an embrace of thighs and arms. He rode her in long heavy strokes, using his massive arms and legs to their best advantage.

They moved with an easy familiarity that soon reached its frantic peak. Her fingers dug into his back, her knees drew up as she brought her heels down to his buttocks, clinging to him with what must have been all her strength.

Her desperate efforts as her passion climbed high carried the Marechal forward, enjoying himself in a way that he had almost forgotten. He thrust into her not just for himself, but for her as well, and with a smile that was lost in the darkness, the scarred man remembered what it was to truly make love and not just the sweaty contortions leading to physical release, quickly forgotten and insignificant.

He felt himself on the brink but withheld himself, never breaking his rhythm, willing himself onward so that she might find her pleasure with his cock deep inside her.

Her heavy breaths came faster then, mingling with whimpers that turned to full throated moans. Her hips bucked against his own, almost to the point of pain as bone butted against bone, but it only made the Marechal grin all the wider.

Then with a jerk, she lifted up off the bed, her spine curving back, her legs stiffening in perfect stillness, all poised, all balanced for one perfect instant before the avalanche.

He felt her then, her pelvis seizing in tight around him and then her legs flexed in heavy spasms that held him tight as he rode her.

His determination crumbled as her orgasm took her from him and the Marechal felt himself drive forward, harder and faster, until with his breath hissing between gritted teeth, his scrotum drew up tight and his cock grew rigid to the point of bursting. Her small hands were holding his sides and the Marechal came inside her. All the muscles of his body rippled like those of a fleet stallion galloping upon a desolate moor, and his cock sprayed into her warmth with undulations that matched her own.

He sagged slightly as his cock continued to jerk with the tremors of his orgasm, and then he heard a familiar voice say, "Well, we done warmed yer bed a'right, I should say."

In that instant it came to the Marechal. The scent of apples and lilacs. He had marked it once before, in the library of House Perene, as the servant woman Melisse brought him his wine.

Her hair had been done up in a tight coiffure unintended to be comely, but practical as befitted the life of a servant. He did not recognize her with those long locks tumbling down her neck, but more than this, he did not recognize the woman he had seen in the manor, one who shrank from the gaze of others. One who visibly wished to make herself as invisible as possible, unwilling to be noticed.

He had not recognized her for the woman who strode so easily into a brothel full of men, some of them dangerous, and did so alone with a confidence that belied some secret strength.

Only the scent of lilacs and apples had disappeared at some point and the air had turned cool.

Upon the bed, he made out the dim features of Harnei, the barmaid from earlier, her sweaty face tilted back with her eyes closed.

The Marechal jumped off the bed and shouted, "Where is she? The woman whose place you took…where did she go?"

The woman merely shook her head and the Marechal rushed to dress himself.

His shirt still unbuttoned, he flew to the corridor and was momentarily blinded by lantern light, but at the end of the narrow passage a window stood open with lace curtains shifting gently in the evening breeze.

The Marechal belted his sword at his waist, dashing to the window beneath which there was a roofed porch at ground level. But even more to his liking, in the distance he caught a glimpse of a shadow disappearing around a corner in a narrow alleyway. A shadow that moved as though panicked.

The next instant saw the scarred man rising from the ground, earthenware roof tiles tumbled around him. Instead of serving as a convenient stepping stone from the upstairs window to the ground below, the little porch roof had ceded under the Marechal's weight, its structure in ruins as he burst forward to chase after a shadow.

His long legs carried him down deserted streets, too narrow for any but those on foot, and at each turning, in the corner of his eye, he thought he saw a flap of a cloak, or dark hair billowing then disappearing just as quickly.

He loped forward, confident. The glimpses grew more frequent as he gained upon the fleeing woman. He guessed that while she did not seem to tire, her panic was forcing her to turn in every direction but the one that would let her escape him.

They ran down closer to the small river that divided the quarter. The Marechal could smell it and under that odor there was the scent of blood and bone.

Finally, he turned a last corner and saw her. She had stopped, appearing to look back in his direction and as he came into view, she fled once again, this time across a small footbridge spanning the water.

Her feet made no sound upon the wooden bridge and the Marechal followed suit. In front of them both loomed a large building that appeared to be built directly into the stony embankment. He watched her slip behind a door to disappear within.

He did not hesitate to follow, fearing no ambush, and as he did the odors of animals and fear assaulted him. He stood still, listening. The air was noticeably cooler here and the Marechal believed he knew what the building was.

He smiled. The woman he had hunted all this time had run out of choices. There would be no back door through which she could escape.

The Marechal walked calmly forward, taking his time, and then he had it. There was the faintest trace of apples and lilacs in the gloom, there where all else reeked of bloodletting and death.

He followed his nose into the darkness only to have the feeling that the space around him had suddenly grown larger. The quality of sound had changed and he could hear water dripping somewhere nearby.

There was a flash that put spots before his eyes, then he saw her as she placed a lit torch back in its socket on the wall.

They were in an abattoir. The windowed building front gave way to cold rooms carved into the hillside running along the riverfront. Here men had found a means of cooling meat quickly before salting, with all the water necessary to wash away the stink of their work.

The walls on three sides were of solid rock made of what appeared to be limestone, only instead of creamy white, much of it was stained a horrid brown or black and large hooks hung suspended from an iron track that ran along the stone ceiling.

And there was the woman named Melisse looking down at the floor. Her arms were crossed across her chest and when she looked up at the Marechal, her eyebrows were knitted angrily together.

"Why can't you leave me alone?" she asked, then continued, "I simply don't have the time for this. I am being hunted and I can hardly stay ahead."

The Marechal smiled as he said, "Yes, I admit that I have been on your trail for quite a while, Melisse. But please, there is no more need for panic. My only wish is to find out the truth of what you know concerning the death of Olivier Perene, among other things. However, I don't accuse you. I have never believed you responsible, for that matter, but I think you can help me in more ways than one."

The relief he expected to see on her worried face did not appear. If anything, it looked as though she grew angrier.

"No, you stubborn, ridiculous man. I made a mistake and thought to rest a moment among other people, just for a brief time. And there you were. I had to be sure. But there is danger following me. I can feel it."

Her voice softened as she said, "I ran from you to protect you, Marechal."

He opened his mouth then closed it again, trying to decide what to think of her words when the sound of thunder hammered through the abattoir, shaking the stone beneath their feet.

A day's journey to the north, along an old, little used track, there was a small cottage with a small vegetable garden just out front.

The soil had been partially turned not long before and where it had not, a few weeds stubbornly held fast.

Inside the cottage, an elderly man held his elderly wife in his arms and together they wept silent tears.

His were for the morrow that they would yet live to see.

Hers were for those whom there would be no next day, not if the doom that had just passed by turned its many eyed gaze upon them.

Melisse heard the sound that was not thunder rolling through the cavernous space of the abattoir. With it was the sound, somehow musical, of hundreds of windows shattering to tinkle down in thousands upon thousands of shards.

Silence followed for the space of an instant, then the mournful notes of flutes playing in a dirge drifted to her ears. It was delicate in its way, only a half step from being true music. She thought that if it had been just slightly closer to real melody, it would have been enough to break the living heart beating within her chest.

There came the muffled wingbeats of hundreds of birds and as she turned to look beyond the Marechal, she saw pure, blinding white snow that moved in near silence.

She watched as everything slowed to a crystalline scale. The handsome man before her, with his jagged scar that only made his appearance more rugged in its beauty, this magnificent man spun round, his sword appearing in his hands as if by magic while the pure white of hundreds of downy wings bore down upon him.

There were eyes as well. Rainbow colors that danced and flashed like summer dragonflies, hundreds of them amongst the wings and she could hear mourning in the thing's breath, singing its dirge as it swept forward.

The Marechal struck first, his blade flashing like a lightning bolt and the winged beast simply divided itself, flowing around the edge of his weapon as it passed.

Sparks flew, like those at a smith's anvil, and then the swordsman was turning, coming round to strike again.

Melisse saw feathers wafting into the air, and she was struck once more by their resemblance to snow. Like the thick, cottony flakes that float upon winter's winds, when the cold shows some little mercy for the sake of beauty.

As they fell, some of them struck the man wielding his sword from side to side, and where they touched him, they sank in as if he were made of butter.

Thick red blood pattered from his wounds to the floor as he struck out with his blade over and over again.

A feather brushed Melisse's arm as it fell and she watched, frozen, as her skin slipped open along a line almost too thin to see. When she jerked her arm back from the plume's touch, red welled up in a wound that was as clean as if a razor had divided her flesh.

She could hear a woman screaming as she watched the Marechal battle the creature. He was losing ground and the floor beneath his feet was slick with his own blood.

His shirt had fallen to blood-splotched tatters and his skin was riddled in long slices that wept in burgundy.

The creature seethed and shifted around the sword thrusts that came faster and faster. Sweeping arcs that no man could sustain for long, not while bleeding his life's blood out onto the abattoir's floor.

She watched as the monster drew itself back, seeming to gather itself. The Marechal hesitated, his notched blade held before him as his torso and thighs streamed rivulets of blood.

The feathered creature retreated and seemed to condense in some way that Melisse could feel. The air was being drawn palpably back. With no warning, her head was in a vise. Her ears popped as she clapped both hands to her head, a pain like an ice pick sinking between her eyes.

Then the air around the monster rolled in a visible wave and there was a sound that rode its crest toward the man doing what he could to protect her.

The heavy rolling sound of thunder was bound in that wave, and behind that, a high-pitched tone of woodwinds that arced into the Marechal's body.

An explosion enveloped the man and then propelled him like a child's doll to crash into a cold stone wall.

The air stank of sulfur and blood. Melisse saw that the floor was cracked where the Marechal had stood. He lay across from her, unmoving, crumpled and broken.

She had seen the force that had thrown him there. Enough to have shattered every bone in his beautiful body and her thought was that she was grateful she had known the touch of his lips before it was too late.

The white monstrosity turned to her, its feathers seething in a mass that shone like gemstones. It eyed her with its hundreds of glittering eyes, reflecting colors in prisms that belonged to another realm.

She felt the floor under her feet shake for the third time, accompanied by a hollow thump, and a second monster appeared to join the first.

It had a lizard's body, mottled in dull browns and greens. Six legs supported it as it whirled to face the feathered demon. Nearly as long as two men, it moved with a fluid grace that reminded Melisse of a hunting cat. Around its long torso, there was a thin metal chain that wrapped it in shining silver.

The demon on six legs turned to look at her before its lips peeled back in what Melisse thought was a smile. Only that infernal grin was lined in dozens of needlelike fangs with bits of leather or skin hanging from between them.

With a squeal like a frightened pig, the feathered demon retreated before the other as it reared up on two legs, while its other four clawed talons dropped to the silver chain working at some hidden clasp.

There was a slithering sound and the metal binding drifted to the floor in loose, shining loops. With an awkward sort of hop, the lizard-like beast freed itself from the loops only to reach down and take a length of the chain in its claws.

It remained standing on two legs, counterbalanced by its long tail lying flat behind it. And it began to undulate its body while the chain began to spin in its four-clawed grip.

Melisse was reminded of the *jongleurs* she had seen that traveled through the region, able to do amazing things with bottles and knives, tossing them into the air in complicated patterns that seemed to defy all possibility.

The grinning beast was just like that. Its four claws had the chain in its grip and turned it around, almost delicately, until it began to spin. And soon the chain was spinning in time with the rippling torsions of its body, paying out to form a shining circle that whistled as it cut the air.

The feathered demon shrank down as it watched and Melisse believed she could see fear in its many-eyed gaze. The white feathers of its body trembled as it hesitated before the other beast and the chain it wielded.

It shrank down, smaller, tighter, and then with a violent shudder, the feathered demon exploded into hundreds of separate wings, each crowned in a single rainbow eye that gleamed as they flew forward.

At first, the whirling chain was terrible in its efficiency. When the small white wings flew into it, they burst and shattered, their gemstone eyes falling dim to the abattoir's floor.

Except that they numbered in the hundreds as the white wings pounded their way into the beast's weapon, trying to foul the whistling shield. Crystalline plumes rained down and Melisse saw that they cut the six legged demon where they chanced to fall upon it. She saw deep ragged wounds appear that seeped a thick blue, what she supposed was its blood.

In time, the chain began to break under the onslaught of the white beast that was not one beast, but hundreds capable of flaying flesh at the slightest touch.

The lizard paid out more and more of its silver chain, pieces breaking away to fall uselessly to the floor. Finally, there were wings that had managed to penetrate its defenses and the lizard was quickly in the midst of a swarm of sparkling white.

The brown demon dropped down to all six legs, spinning and jerking as the wings attacked it. But Melisse saw that it had no intention of retreating when it reared back up, this time with pieces of broken chain in each of its four clawed talons. It flailed them about in four directions, batting down wings like summer moths to shatter on the floor. The demon hammered relentlessly at them on all sides with a pounding rhythm like thunder and war drums.

It streamed blue blood, but the onslaught of white destruction began to slow as the floor was littered in broken plumes and rainbow eyes that saw no more.

In a rushing wind, the remaining unbroken wings flew back from the flailing lizard, coalescing once more into a single white monstrosity, only now much diminished.

The brown demon advanced, its needle grin stretching ever wider, and then Melisse heard the terrible sound of breaking glass that seemed to stretch on for an eternity.

Behind the feathered beast, a golden crack appeared in the air and it widened into an opening. Beyond, there was golden fire that blazed in a realm unknown to men. One that Melisse recognized as the corridors of light and flame in which she had once chanced to travel.

The white demon gathered itself and as it broke away, making for the doorway it had opened, a last length of silver chain lashed out, wrapping around the beast as it squealed in fury and fear.

The six legged demon momentarily held it back from escape by the chain clasped in its claws. But the feathered demon made an ultimate effort and Melisse watched as the lizard was dragged forward, skidding across the stone floor.

She saw both demons slip through the crack in reality, one of them squealing its rage while the other trailed behind it, grinning and bleeding blue.

The opening slammed shut with a booming reverberation and all fell to silence.

It was almost beautiful to watch as a last few feathers wafted lazily down, but the beauty was deadly, spoiled by the destruction and violence of its razored edges.

Melisse carefully made her way over to the Marechal's body, not knowing what else to do.

He was on his side and she could see that the blood had stopped trickling from his countless wounds.

She went to her knees and reached out a trembling hand to touch the scar that ran down his body. It started at his jaw and then plunged down across his blood-splattered torso in jagged lines that reminded her of lightning blazing down from the heavens.

Except that she could see his bare back, drenched red in spilled blood, and the scar was there as well, its lines matching that of the other side. Her breath caught as she tried to imagine what kind of violence could have done such a thing. Whatever it had been, it had cut the man nearly in two like a log split for the hearth. A wound so cataclysmic that no one could have survived.

Her eyes stung then, as she considered how valiantly he had fought, interposing himself between her and the monster, giving it no thought as he made of himself a shield between her and death.

And that he had paid the ultimate price against a being that should never have existed except in the nightmare of fever dreams.

She tugged at him, rolling the Marechal's body onto his back. She wanted to see his face a last time before she left to take up her journey once more.

His eyes were closed and he seemed at peace. Almost as though he were only resting.

Melisse dared what she had not in his life and put her arms around him to rest her head upon his broad chest.

Only to jump up just as quickly, her mouth dropping open.

"That's…that's not possible," she said to no one, then put her head down to listen once more.

There it was again. Not just one heartbeat, but two, a second one behind the first, fainter, smaller, but there all the same.

Then she felt heavy muscles moving under her as his ribcage expanded to take a deep breath.

Melisse lifted her head up and she saw his eyes slitted open, looking at her, his mouth upturned in amusement.

With a cough, the Marechal pushed himself erect and said, "Yes, I know. It happens that I am particularly difficult to kill."

Her eyes widened as she said, "But your heart...I mean, hearts. You have two...."

The scarred man chuckled as he said, "Not two, not really. Rather, it's just the one that healed a little too quickly into two halves. I admit, for a time the sound of it in my chest was disconcerting, but after all these years I've gotten used to it."

Melisse stammered, "But that's not possible."

"Nevertheless," he replied, "Melisse, do you remember the conversation I had with Lord Perene in the library? Concerning the legend of the Alchemist of Urrune and his assistant?"

"Yes," she said, slowly, "Lord Perene mentioned a name. I think it was Etienne...Etienne St. Lucq."

The Marechal sighed as he got to his feet, swaying slightly as he did.

"That's right. While I've gone by many names over the years, the one given me at birth is Etienne St. Lucq. The Alchemist of Urrune was my father."

Her voice shook with astonishment as she said, "But that was three hundred years ago."

"Three hundred and eight years, to be precise," he replied.

Outside the slaughterhouse, a small crowd had gathered. Onlookers peered through the broken windows and facade, intent to see what had been the source of the explosions that had shaken the entire quarter.

Among them was a poorly dressed man. One might have imagined him as someone fallen on hard times. Someone whose skin hung upon him, a very corpulent man who had lost a great deal of weight and done so too quickly.

He peered over the shoulders of the bystanders then stepped back, his eyes shifting from side to side in their sockets, the skin loose and sagging.

With a lurching clumsy gait, he shuffled away as the crowd leaned in to see the bloodied man and woman limping out of the darkness, leaning heavily on one another as they came.

The End

The Marechal Chronicles continues with the following prequel story, previously published separately.

THE GOBLIN BETWEEN HER THIGHS

An army captain with a mysterious scar is torn from the battlefront and from his lover in this story of espionage, body thieves, and devious eroticism.

The legendary Goblin War rages on while Alexandre's own identity slips away from him in his struggle between his forgotten past and the woman who loves him. Action, intrigue, and intense sexuality…all this and more await between these pages.

This is a prequel to the events recounted in the ongoing series, The Marechal Chronicles. The story takes place one hundred and fifty years prior to the Marechal's involvement with Melisse and the events surrounding her.

They were alone. At least, as alone as could be expected in the middle of an army, one that was camped under a pouring rain at the edge of a dread forest.

Sounds of coughing, of armor creaking, and of mud sucking at soldiers' feet as they tramped by infiltrated the canvas tent, but the man and the woman within felt at peace and far removed from the corpse-strewn battlefield of just a few days before.

It was a soldier's life, those few moments stolen in desperation until the next maneuver found them thrust back into the living sea of military men and women crashing wave after wave upon the rocks that were their enemy, the goblin hoard of old.

Black blood and ichor had stained the hands of both of them. Hands that now touched one another in tenderness as the man brought his lips to drink at those of the woman.

She moved under him, her body as naked as his, not in denial, but in motions of desire and welcome.

The kiss lingered upon their lips as they broke contact and he dipped his head to run his mouth along her neck, drifting as light as a feather to behind her ear where he knew she was especially vulnerable to his touch.

Her hair was of steel, where his showed no sign of grey. But her body was trim and muscular, the body of a career soldier who took every aspect of her metier to its logical extreme.

He could read discipline in her least gesture, even in the smile she gave him as he pulled back from nuzzling her neck. It was why he was so drawn to her. That she was a mature woman was part of it as well.

He did not remember his mother, and only very little of his father, and supposed that therein lay some echo of the missing puzzle pieces of his past.

"Alexandre, I need you inside me," she whispered, her tone as direct as ever.

He replied, "And who asks? My general, or my lover?"

"Both…neither…only make love to me, soldier." Her voice rose as she opened her thighs to him.

He dropped his head down to her heavy breasts and took a dark nipple into his mouth. She tasted of lye soap, the best one could expect in a simple life spent marching from one battlefield to the next, most often passing weeks at a time with no chance to wash, much less bathe.

That she was now a general changed little in the way of privileges, although the two of them would not deny in that moment, a general's personal quarters, a small tent meant just for her, was welcome enough.

He ran his hands down her body. Her skin was soft despite her hard life.

"Now, Alexandre," she urged him.

He lifted up and slipped into the moist warmth between her thighs with a sigh.

They had known each other in this way at every opportunity, during each stolen moment. And it was with that easy sense of familiarity that he moved gently against her as she wrapped her legs around him.

Two bodies rocked in counterpoint, creating a steady rhythm that found its cadence quickly. They thrust against each other, forcing themselves to clash when all they desired was to be in harmony.

Their breaths came faster and the steel-haired woman moaned with her pleasure. The sound brought a smile to the man's face, a profoundly handsome visage marred only by a scar that traced a vicious path along his jawline and down his torso.

Her breath quickened and he could feel her begin to arch up off the simple pallet they used for a bed. He continued his rhythmic thrusting with no break in the movement, wishing only that she reach her utmost pleasure.

Small hands flew to his back., Fingers that were most at ease around a sword's hilt gripped him and pulled him tight to her as her hips buffeted in the wind of orgasm. She cried out, but softly, her thighs hitching around him in heavy spasms.

Her pleasure rolled through him and he could feel her clenching around him. It was enough to carry him to the brink and he let himself tumble over the edge, his buttocks seizing hard as he blew into her, a sea born tempest crashing upon her shores.

There was sweat upon her brow as he kissed her tenderly above her steel grey eyes. The taste of soap was now mingled with that of salt, and the thought of ocean storms in lovemaking seemed to him just as apt as ever.

They rolled onto their sides and she reached up to touch the scar that ran along his face.

"Alexandre, who are you?" she asked, her voice heavy in the warmth that enveloped them.

"What do you mean?" he asked.

She sighed and said, "I mean that we have lain together for more than two years, Captain, and I still don't know the story of this scar. You tell me nothing and I doubt, even, that Alexandre is your name."

He moved away from her then. It was not the first time that she had broached the subject, but never had she been so direct.

"Is it not a fact that when a man or woman joins the soldier lists the past life is wiped away? That who we were before does not follow us into the ranks and together we define ourselves through action and bravery?" he asked.

"Yes. It is true. There are criminals, or husbands and wives who have shorn their ties with families, people who have left behind all that they know," she said.

"And," he interrupted, "No one is given leave to pry at that past, not even a general."

She waited as his words hung in the air. She had not wanted it to go this way. Not now, so soon before what would come upon the morrow.

"I do not ask as a general, Alexandre. I ask as your lover."

He sat up and that he distanced himself further was not lost upon her.

The lightning strike path of the scar was clear in the dim light of a camp lantern. Its jagged track was visible down his back as much as it was upon his front, the remnant of what must have been a terribly grievous wound.

Except that she had known him from the time he entered military service and, by consequence, the war. The scar had marked him already and she could not help but think that it was at the heart of all he did to turn his back so resolutely upon his previous life.

What was visible upon that muscular body was not the only scar. The large man who shared her bed carried another that ran just as deeply on the inside.

"And you," he said over his shoulder to her, "Is your name really Sandrine, General Grise?"

His voice had become clipped in tone, the voice of a soldier responding to a superior officer.

"Alexandre, don't do this…not now," she said to his scarred back.

He shrugged and stood up from the bed. His captain's uniform was slung over the single chair in the tent, and he wasted no time in dressing himself.

"Why does it feel so much like an interrogation then, Sandrine? Why does it sound like distrust?" he asked as he buckled his belt and adjusted the heavy blade scabbarded at his side.

She hung her head, and he took that as her answer as he opened the flap that served as the entrance of the tent and stepped out into the night.

The rain still fell, and it ran down his grim face like tears as he made his way toward the huddled forms of soldiers gathered around low campfires.

A messenger boy scratched at the open tent flap, and the captain motioned for him to enter.

"Captain!" The messenger snapped a salute to the seated man who wrapped his hands around a tin cup. The bitter odor of boiled coffee hung in the morning air.

"What is it, then?" the scarred man asked without looking up.

The messenger dropped the hand held rigidly to his brow and said, "Captain, you have been convoked to the rear of the army. Your presence is required immediately at the hospital wagons."

Alexandre groaned. If he had been called to the hospital wagons, it meant that General Blanc had died or was at death's door. It would be a hard blow to the army's morale, already low upon hearing that a goblin giant had shattered the man's legs with a single blow while ahorse at the last battlefront.

The general was among the eldest of the military leaders and when he fell, it was if an old friend had been stricken down. He was possessed of an uncommon charisma, and that he always put himself in the way of danger, as much as any common soldier, had endeared him to them all. He was their father and his passing would not be overlooked. Already the other generals had taken the initiative to reorganize and behaved as though the old man had never been.

It was an army's way. No man was indispensable, no single life could compromise the whole.

"Alright," the captain said, standing up, "Lead the way."

An army surgeon greeted him at the front of the hospital tent.

"How is General Blanc?" asked the captain, fearing to hear the worst.

The surgeon smiled as he walked with the captain. "Better than he has any right to be. Old fella's one tough bit of leather, it would seem."

Instead of leading him directly into the large tent of the wounded and dying, the surgeon marched around the exterior of the impromptu hospital to a smaller tent set back and away from the unrelenting sounds of men and women in terrible pain.

"We had to take one of his legs, which should have meant the end for him, but the General has other ideas about that."

The surgeon pointed to the smaller tent before them, "He's in there,"

"You're not his first visitor today, nor, I suppose, his last. But don't tax the man. While any immediate danger has been averted, I don't want him overtired. He needs to heal and I can promise you that you wouldn't be here if he hadn't insisted on it."

The scarred captain nodded and stepped inside the dark interior.

His first sense was that he did not smell the sickening sweet odor of rot that was just as fatal as a sword thrust to the heart. He waited for his eyes to adjust to the gloomy interior while real hope that General Blanc would live bloomed in his heart.

"Ah, Captain No One...thank you for coming."

The voice was weak but unmistakable. And for once, Alexandre did not mind the joke that had followed him throughout all his military days. He had been dubbed "No One" by General Blanc himself. Two years ago, Alexandre had presented himself to the inscription rolls in a faraway city, and when the lieutenant secretary asked him his name, he had responded, "No one." The General had been nearby and upon hearing those words, he had marched straight over and cocked an ear to what was being said.

The lieutenant insisted on having Alexandre's name, and when the scarred man refused to even make up an alias, the general laughed and said, "You heard the man, Lieutenant. He said he's no one and that's just what you'll record. No one."

And with a wink, he added, "Any man with a scar like that and still walking around is a man I want on my side of the battlefield when the time comes. Welcome to my army, No One."

The name was pinned on him that day and had stayed with him ever since.

"General!" said the captain, snapping to a rigid salute before the old man lying on top of an army cot, the outline of his blankets showing the hollow where one of his legs should have been.

"At ease, Captain."

"Alexandre," he continued, "I've sent the other generals away. They know most of what this is about. Hell, there are so few I can trust and they're the ones who brought me the names of the men and women we need for this, and you were among them."

Alexandre remembered the strange behavior of Sandrine the night before.

"But the rest of it needs to stay quiet. It needs to stay secret and if I die, most of the secret dies with me and all of you will be safe."

"General, if I may, but safe from what?" asked the captain.

The old man appeared to hesitate, weighing what he would say next, then said, "It was no coincidence that we took such heavy losses in the last battle, Captain. The goblins don't fight that way. They never have…until now.

"There was intelligence in what they did. There was calculation and strategy. Bloody hell, they knew what *we* were going to do."

The captain guessed what the general would say next, but it still surprised him.

"We've been infiltrated, Captain. There is no way of knowing who it is, who we can trust.

"The few wizards we have left tell me that there is some precedent in the annals. Once before when goblins waged war on humanity, there was mention of someone or something that taught them how to wear the skins of men. A way to take the place of those they killed and become undetectable spies."

It was as though someone had punched him in his guts. The scarred captain sucked air and could not catch his breath. Goblins were horrid fighters, tough and scaled creatures that were almost impossible to kill. But they had never shown themselves capable of any organization or strategy, let alone devious plans such as outright espionage.

"What we do know," the old general continued, "is that the information they are gleaning has come from very high up, the topmost echelons.

"You and your cohorts, of whom you will have no firsthand knowledge, will be stripped of rank and will leave this army to travel to all corners of the empire. Anonymous, each of you shall enter into the family service belonging to our generals and you will lie there in wait, watching and waiting. It is up to each of you to root the bastards out and kill them where they stand.

"Our hope is that as our high level officers take temporary leave of the army for standard family visits, they will reveal themselves in some way or another, there where they will be less on their guard within their own homes."

Alexandre stood there, frozen, as the truth of what was happening slowly sank in.

"There were some who voiced doubt in choosing you to be part of this," said the general, "But your skill with a blade is well known, Captain No One, and I trust you.

"Prove me right and make your sword sing like it never has before wherever you find them."

That afternoon Alexandre left behind his uniform and the rest of his military accoutrements. His horse was saddled with standard tack of modest but utilitarian make. He had waited then, hesitating, but when no familiar face came to see him off, he was reminded of the general's words, that there were those who doubted Alexandre. His indecision vanished.

And as he rode farther and farther away from the army that had been his home for so long, he realized that the holes of his memory had not been filled in no matter how much death he had dealt out upon the battlefield.

He rode from the unknown into the unknown, which made him smile with a mouth that held no humor. Sandrine had asked her questions, not knowing who he really was. But her doubts would not have been assuaged if she had learned that he was his own mystery and remained unknown even to himself.

Lorenna watched her mistress upon the parapet. A cold wind had risen up out of the valley below and it raked its hard fingers through the noblewoman's hair. She was blond, a rare color more akin to autumn and harvested wheat and not the chill, bare days before spring finally broke to sweep the winter back from whence it came.

For now though, the forest to the west remained a grey jagged thing, unadorned in the greenery that would soften it and make of it a verdant carpet lying in the distance. Her mistress braved the cold as she did each day, the color drained from her skin while she searched the horizon for some sign of him.

It had been more than a year since the master of the house had been summoned to war. He had spent his younger days training as a military man before coming back to inherit the family home at the death of his father. There was wealth enough to keep the demesne in security and comfort, but no amount of money could turn the winds of war when it rose.

He was made a general, they had heard, but little else. They only knew that the war did not go well and the fear that goblins would overrun the empire was rampant.

Lorenna wanted to be brave like her mistress, who stood in the worst of the cold air searching, ever searching for his return. But she was only a handmaiden of noble blood too diluted to provide her with the courage that she needed in such fell times.

Instead, each day she mounted the tower steps with her mistress and accompanied her to the doorway that opened out to the parapet overlooking the surrounding countryside. She admired the determination that she read in the straight back of the woman before her, her long yellow tresses trailing in the wind like gay streamers belonging to merrier times.

She tried to do her best, but each time, Lorenna did not find strength enough to stand at her mistress's side and cast her own gaze upon the grey lands so far below. She simply contented herself at the doorway, worrying that with each passing day the noblewoman bowed little by little under the weight of her husband's absence.

As it was, her mistress had become terribly distant, no longer taking Lorenna into her confidences. One day, before the past winter had seized all in ice and snow, her mistress had commanded her horse made ready and had ridden to the verges of the grey forest. She had refused all accompaniment, even if that would have only amounted to the young man in the stables. Lorenna remained suspicious of him and counseled against it, despite there being no one else, unless it were the old gatekeeper who had not ridden in twenty years.

The handmaiden considered the man in their livery of doubtful origins, most likely a deserter from the war as his dreadful scar appeared to attest. That he was otherwise comely only counted further against him in her eyes, and so it was that the noblewoman rode out alone that day.

Except that what should have been a short ride turned to a dreadful nightmare when she did not return until after dark. The few women in the kitchens had joined Lorenna as she paced from one end of the great hall to the other, wondering what to do. In the past, her mistress would ride for an hour or two, always skirting the forest's edge. In her heart, Lorenna knew that her mistress hoped to find her husband riding to her, as in a lovely tale of princes and princesses, up out of the dark forest and into her welcoming arms.

When night had fallen and Lorenna had nearly made up her mind to seek out the help of the scarred stableman, they had heard the clopping of horse hooves upon the cobbled road of the chateau.

She was there and chilled to the bone, her blond hair soaked through as if she had ridden through a tempest. Despite all their questions of how it came to be that she was dripping wet on a dry calm evening, her mistress remained silent and shaking even after they had raised a great fire in the largest fireplace of the demesne.

The noblewoman spoke no words and shivered for what seemed an eternity to Lorenna. When the next day finally came, she found her mistress calm but with invisible walls surrounding her, and she offered no explanation for the night before. She seemed to have taken the cold deep inside her and that temperament remained a barrier to any warmth shown to her ever after.

Politesse and etiquette held their place in the chateau and the noblewoman remained faithful to that. But the whispered confidences or simple pleasantries that the women told one another had come to an end that night.

Lorenna watched as her mistress tirelessly scanned the horizon. Sometimes the handmaiden wondered if the lord of the house might have been killed in the war. So many had died and now there were so few men under the chateau's roof. Most had heard the call of war and answered it in the way of men. They left their women, their children, and their elders and went off to die before the butchery of monsters who saw no value in life and expended themselves with no thought to their own preservation.

A human answer to inhuman destruction. It seemed to her worse than an injustice that an able-bodied man worked in safety in the chateau's stables while so many others lay dead upon far battlefields. She had tried questioning him and how he had come by such an evil looking scar, but the he and his gruff manner had rebuffed her at every turn. When Lorenna had approached her mistress with the idea that the new stablehand should be turned out, her mistress simply replied that they had need of him and that she would hear no more on the matter.

Lorenna had felt foolish then, as she had been the one that pleaded to let him in when he came knocking upon their gate, almost a beggar but for the horse he rode.

As she considered these thoughts, Lorenna saw that the noblewoman had lifted her hands to the stone wall before her. Her fingers gripped the frigid stone and her knuckles whitened with the strain.

She began to rise up on her toes and, with a cry, Lorenna rushed forward, sure that the lady meant to fall and put an end to the misery of her solitude.

Instead, she turned to the handmaiden and for an instant Lorenna thought she saw raw hunger and violence in the woman's shining eyes before her features softened into a careful smile, saying, "Lorenna, my dear friend. He comes. My husband returns from war."

She looked past her mistress and there, far below to where she had never dared to look before, rode a tiny figure slumped upon a stumbling horse. He looked like a child's lead figurine, a toy soldier far too small to be of consequence, much less real.

Together, the two women descended the winding stairs and called to the gatekeeper to raise the barred portcullis, that which lay between them and the savagery of the exterior world.

The nobleman's eyes, now those of a general, were tired and vacant. His armor was battered and rusted, his horse ridden near to death.

Lorenna tried hard to remember him as he had been the day he rode out and away from the chateau. The sun had been shining, she was sure of that, and the men who rode with him carried bright banners that trailed behind them with the brash pride of those who knew of war only from books and lessons.

The face she saw now at the great table was lined and weathered. He said he had ridden for days on end when he had been given leave to return home for a short while. But the war went badly and he could not stay long.

The kitchen went to work at once with great fuss and bustle, their efforts now steaming upon the table.

Lorenna watched as the lord devoured piece after piece of guinea fowl, the juices running down his chin. She looked away, then told herself to be brave and that it was impolite, only to see him staring at her over his brimming cup of wine.

His wife spoke gently and of matters of little import. Some few words concerning the meager harvest of the past year, that there were too few men to work the fields or that it was of little consequence because there were also fewer mouths to feed.

He seemed to listen to her, but when next he spoke, it was as though he had been holding his own internal conversation.

"Mankind is losing ground before the onslaught. The goblins have a found a means of infiltrating the ranks of leadership upon the battlefield, leading to bloody ambushes that have been costly to the effort."

"What kind of 'means' have the goblins found against us, dear husband?" his wife asked.

"We remain uncertain, but there are rumors that speak of goblins walking among us, yet unseen, stealing our secrets and strategies for the battlefield," he replied, his lips slick and shining with red wine staining the corners like blood.

Lorenna shuddered upon hearing this.

Her mistress replied, "But how can this be? I thought them but ruthless monsters. Violent and merciless, but certainly lacking in the intelligence needed for such subtleties."

"There are certain stories," he said, "of a few goblins who once exercised this ability in their insatiable lust for the human form. It is the foundation for their hatred of men. They desire our very flesh and the potential for pleasure that they themselves cannot know in their twisted bodies, befouled and inured against the brutality of their rude existence.

"Above all, they utilized this ruse to seduce and know human women in the most carnal of meanings," he finished.

His wife shook her head slowly."I remember the tales my nan would tell me and I no higher than her knees at the time. Stories that told of women being bewitched by goblin magic, waking the next morning to a monster in their beds. I thought them but tales for children."

"Dear wife," he replied, "If I have learned anything in my travails these past two years, it is that our childhood tales walk this world with the blood of men upon their evil faces. There is truth at the heart of those things which we dare not believe, despite our most sincere wish that it were otherwise."

Silence fell then at the dinner table and Lorenna, her own appetite gone, watched as the nobleman crunched thin bones between his teeth to suck out the marrow within.

She was afraid of the dark. As far back as she could remember, Lorenna had always hated being shut up in her bedchamber alone, the comforting glow of beeswax candles snuffed out with no thought to the fears of the child that she had been.

Later, she found the darkness of night less unsettling, but mostly that was due to sharing her bed with other ladies-in-waiting, chastely and in good-humored camaraderie.

Here, though, there were only shadows and forgotten garments to keep her company. The scent of dust was in the air and not the shared laughter of other young women.

Lorenna knew it was wrong, but once she had found it out, she had been drawn to it like a moth to the flame. Her chamber was spacious and at the back, there was an enormous armoire built into the wall, within which she kept her clothing and other sundry affairs. One day, she could not find a particular pair of shoes so she had pushed her way through the hanging garments, searching in the dark and discovered that the armoire had no proper back. Instead, it was a sort of closet that continued in what could be considered a short corridor with a great deal of forgotten attire and cartons that fell apart at the slightest touch. Steeling her courage, Lorenna had forced her way through the forest of wool and linen only to arrive at a wooden door that she recognized immediately. It was the twin of the one belonging to the armoire in her own chamber, only this one opened outward and there before her was the bedchamber of her mistress.

She had jumped back, startled and blushing furiously, making a hasty retreat to her own chamber with her heart hammering in her chest.

Upon a great baldaquin bed, her mistress lay naked. Her skin was of a perfection attributable to the finest porcelain, clear and unblemished. The woman's legs were up and bent at the knees. Her hands were between her thighs and she had been touching herself with small moans coming from between her lips.

Despite herself, Lorenna was soon back at that other door and she pushed it open just enough to see what could be seen. Her mistress was still on her back, only now her hips were shifting back and forth as her fingers plied their way through downy blond hair only a little darker than the woman's golden tresses.

Lorenna had known then that she would be helpless to stop herself from returning over and over to admire her mistress. She knew that no good could ever come of it, this terrible breach of privacy, but the intimacy she knew from within the musty darkness was every bit as addictive as the liquor of the poppy flower, requiring only one taste to trap Lorenna and bring her back time and time again.

The milk-skinned beauty had reached up with one hand to pinch a rosebud nipple while the other hand rubbed in frenzied motions, until, finally, she arched up off the bed with a tiny cry, her thighs flexing with rhythmic spasms.

Lorenna had backed away then, easing the door closed ever so slowly before going back to her chamber, her head spinning and telling herself she would never traverse the armoire again. Never, ever again.

In the months that followed, she had gone back innumerable times, though never chancing upon the same spectacle as that of the first. Most often, she would see the lady at her embroidery or other small tasks. Occasionally, she would see her nude, especially when Lorenna took care to wake very early and be there for when the lady awoke herself.

Then came the misadventure of her mistress's ride to the forest and ever after Lorenna had been deprived. She would see her mistress seated upon the edge of her bed, unmoving, her eyes vacant until finally Lorenna would be close to falling asleep standing up. And for those times that she chanced to be there for the very early morning, she would see the woman still seated in the same position, as if she had not moved a muscle during all the night.

Lorenna knew the idea was preposterous but it unnerved her greatly, and not long after she ceased her secret visitations.

Until now.

She could only imagine the joy that the reunited couple would find that evening in her mistress's bedchamber. The nobleman and his wife, so long parted, so much pent up longing, for one as much as the other.

The shame she felt burning in her face seemed hot enough to illuminate the dark interior of the armoire, but it was still not enough to dissuade the handmaiden. What would ensue this night was too much for Lorenna to withstand. Her mistress would no longer have need of her own hands between her legs. This night, Lorenna would finally see that which men and women do so naturally, and that which she had not yet known for herself.

Her curiosity drew her forward as she pressed a practiced hand to the armoire door, easing it open just enough.

They were there, the nobleman and the lady, upon the bed. He ran his hands down the blond woman's body before coming back up to yank roughly at the crisscrossed cording of her bodice.

Lorenna could understand the urgency of his movements, the two separated after all this time. She did not doubt that he had withheld himself in knowing other women, his fealty intact but wearing thin.

He was feverish as he pulled at her clothing and Lorenna could hear curious sounds. It was almost as though the man growled.

The lady appeared to be in as much haste as her husband as she pushed his hands away, her own fingers springing nimbly to the task of undoing her clothing.

Their mouths were upon one another as they bared their skin. The coverlet of the bed was flung back as the two fell down, writhing against one another like serpents.

Lorenna could feel her heart pounding and she knew her cheeks were flushed red. She could not ignore that there was also heat building between her legs, though this time it was welcome and delicious.

The noblewoman threw her arms up to seize her husband and drag him down upon her. Her thighs wrapped around him and the sound of their lovemaking was bestial in its intensity.

Lorenna's own hand had drifted down to the heavy cloth of her gown, gathering it into a tight ball and forcing it between her legs. Her breaths were deeper, huskier, and she bit her lip around the whimper threatening to escape her.

She watched them, the lord's buttocks pistoning forward, his wife's legs lifting up and seizing around him.

And then, as their contortions became even more frantic, Lorenna saw the serpent.

It came slipping up over the sheets, appearing to move away from the gasping couple, its scaled body shimmering with dun colors. Lorenna nearly screamed as it slithered across the coverlet. That was when she realized that what she took for its narrow head was no head at all. Rather, it was an arrowhead shaped end, in perfect mimicry of the demonic aspect depicted in certain of the chateau's tapestries.

As she watched in horror, it lifted up and she saw then from whence it came. It was a tail and it was attached to the nobleman, its scaled root erupting from the base of his spine.

Her scream lifted in her chest, a great intake of air swelling her lungs when she saw a second one join the first. Instead of a muddy brown color, this one was a murky green. The color reminded her of the muck lying in slack water bogs, and was not so different from the color of her mistress's eyes, once so bright with curiosity and charm, become dim with indifference since that fateful night's ride.

The two pointed tails wrapped around one another and Lorenna understood that the growls and snarls she heard were indeed from two beasts. Two infernal creatures writhing on what had once been her mistress's bed.

She let go her gown, seizing instead an old woolen vest to stuff in her mouth. She bit down hard on the dusty garment. That her very survival was suddenly at stake did not escape her.

Then they spoke. Not with the voices of men and women, but with the gravelly tones of monsters. Those same sounds that come whispering from beneath a child's bed in the dead of night, threatening to bite off the careless foot that left the safety of bedsheets blessed in the hands of good mothers everywhere.

"Not human," said the female, her voice quaking under the violent thrashing of the male between its legs.

"Nor you, my dear," the male replied, "It would seem that our masquerade has fooled even us."

The female grunted with a horrid sound. It reminded Lorenna of someone choking upon bones.

"I have been surrounded by these weaklings for months while biding my time and waiting for the husband to return. I have hungered long to know the flesh of humans in carnal embrace," the blond-haired creature said.

"Aye, and so have I," the male said, "Still, my nose tells me all is not lost."

Suddenly, he pulled back from the female and in a single bound he leapt from the bed with a roar to land before the armoire.

Lorenna held her breath, willing her feet to move, telling herself to flee, to run for her life. Instead, she stood transfixed as the grinning beast wearing a man's skin ripped open the door.

She screamed then, all that she had held back came forth in a shriek that should have shattered every window in the chateau. Her feet broke free as well, but before she could take more than a single shuffling step backward, the creature wrapped a clammy hand around her wrist.

With a wicked grin, he said, "We *shall* know this human girl. She is fresh. She is unspoiled."

"And she is ours," finished the other beast, its mouth lifting into a rictus of a grin that stretched far too wide to be anything but evil incarnate.

Lorenna shrieked again, believing her throat ruptured with fright as the male dragged her across the floor. Her legs failed her as she slumped down, seeing the two cocks wagging stiffly from the beast's pelvis. One pink and smooth skinned, the other black and scaled. Then her mind failed her as well, and all went dark.

Her shoulders ached with a pain unlike any she had ever known. She had been dreaming the worst dream and in her contortions of sleep she had somehow turned both her arms over her head, wrenching them in their sockets.

She could feel a draught and it seemed that she was being rocked like a baby.

Lorenna opened her eyes slowly, not yet sure the nightmare was well and truly over, only to see the leering faces of her mistress and the lady's husband. They were both naked and their bodies betrayed no flaw, except that both of them trailed long, sinuous goblin tails from between their buttocks. The male walked with two cocks rigid and bowed in bulging tumescence. One was a black, twisted thing, like the root of a tree that drank at the poisonous waters of a deadman's swamp; the other, pink and red, suffused with the color of a man, but inhabited by the will of a monster.

Lorenna tried to inhale for the shriek that was about to erupt from her throat, but she found her mouth stuffed full of something, probably wool torn from some garment. Her arms were over her head, but separated. One was bound in rope to the chandelier, the other wrapped in a ripped coverlet that stretched high to the chamber's sculpted fireplace.

The effect was that she was suspended in midair, her feet only slightly off the ground, and her arms were stretched out and above her in opposite directions.

The being that she had taken for her mistress these past few months was lying on the stone floor at Lorenna's feet. She stared idly up at her, a long tongue snaking out between red, swollen lips.

"What do I see, but a little bird, a baby bird, hiding in its tree." The female's voice was a hideous mix of woman and beast as she spoke.

"I see it peeking, in its little nest, a baby's nest, down at me," it continued.

"So I stretched my neck, cracked my claws.

"And I crunched it down, quick in my maw.

"Its blood so slick and pleasing,

"And then there was no more little bird, no baby bird, peeking down at me."

The female's tongue grew in length and Lorenna could do nothing as she watched the thing go to its knees while reaching up with her mistress's small, gentle hands to force her legs wide.

At first, she felt only hot breath, like that of a rabid dog, then those red lips were nuzzling at the folds between her legs. Lorenna screamed through the wadding in her mouth, but the sound did not carry.

That long, sinuous tongue slipped down her cleft and Lorenna's scream twisted into a moan. The feeling was of intense heat stroking within her folds and despite herself, Lorenna felt her hips flexing in response.

It would mean damnation. She would burn for eternity, she knew, as the creature lapped at her lips and evoked her most hidden desires.

To dream of another woman was against all natural things. But Lorenna knew it was the essence of goblins and the corruption they carried with them. All that they touched withered, all that they did ended in desolation.

Then she could feel something slipping lower, something pushing at her. It took little imagination to picture that snakelike tongue slithering out to explore her opening.

Lorenna tried to squeeze her legs together, to stop the horrid invasion, except that her juices ran thick and she could feel how heavy she had grown down there.

It was detestable. It was wrong. And in that moment, her hips undulating to the rhythm of the creature's lapping tongue, Lorenna desired it more than anything.

A rough hand seized one of her legs at the ankle and it was no small, soft grasp. Rather, it was a hand that knew the hafts of battle axes that cleaved all that lay in their path.

The male goblin laughed and lifted her leg high as he ran his other hand down her thigh.

She was being stretched far too wide, the pain in her shoulders forgotten as her hips stretched to the breaking point. Then the female's lolling tongue slipped inside her, deep inside her, and Lorennna let out a muffled groan.

She had imagined this moment in a thousand different ways. Sometimes with comely young men, even those who carried vicious scars, or more often, with green-eyed women coiffed in long blond braids that were as soft as silk.

But never had she imagined that her maidenhood would be broken in the clasp of goblins.

The female began thrusting its inhuman tongue, grown thick and rigid, deep into Lorenna. And with each forward motion, red lips would buffet against the raised kernel at her apex.

Pain mingled with pleasure in the most profound ways. She could do nothing to stop them. She was theirs to use as they would until she was broken and of no further worth.

She moved with that tongue buried deep inside her and it was not in protest. She moved with the heat that mounted from deep inside, a heat that burned her from within, forcing her to respond as the muscles in her thighs tightened of their own accord.

Lorenna felt the delicious tension winding in tight at her abdomen, her cunt slick and swollen as the goblin pounded its face against her. Her breath came in ragged gasps, threatening to choke her entirely, and when it all became too much, far too much, the dam broke and the flames of orgasm washed through her.

All that she saw doubled, then trebled. Her mind shrank down to a pinpoint that burst to a flaming sun as pleasure ripped through her in great, jagged waves.

The goblin male laughed again, his deep voice reverberating in the bedchamber, but if he said anything, Lorenna could not tell. Her body bounced and jittered in rhythmic spasms. And with each clenching of muscles, another wave of pleasure and pain flooded her until she thought she might die.

With a mighty heave of its free arm, the male seized the other by her hair and ripped her away from Lorenna.

The tongue that had been so deeply embedded inside her hung, twisted slowly, twining down the creature's chin as it grinned its hideous, overlarge grin.

"My turn," the male grated as he positioned himself between Lorenna's legs.

She remembered then the two cocks sprouting from his crotch and the screams that had been at bay for a time came back to burst against the wool stuffed inside Lorenna's mouth.

There was pressure, a terrible pressure that pushed at her in two places at once.

One hole was running free with juices that sprang from her spasming fount, the other was slick with the goblin drool that had gathered there. In either case, there would be no stopping him, a monster without mercy. With a snarl, he forced himself inside her.

Lorenna felt one opening, so recently forced wide, yield easily, while the other back between her buttocks felt as though it was being ripped apart, the black-scaled root tapping into her back passage.

The pain was immense but the goblin did not care, its leering face distorted and shifting as it plunged into her. To her horror, Lorenna could see the creature's eyes, like dark pools of oblivion, swimming behind those of the man who had been named a general upon the field of battle. A man who had lost his life to a slip-skin monster that was as ruthless as it was cunning.

His thrusting became frenzied and Lorenna burned as his two cocks slammed into her over and over again. The pleasure she had felt earlier was gone, replaced by a torment meant for the depths of damnation, and she wondered if she might have already stepped beyond death's door without knowing it.

Then the female goblin hissed and jumped backwards, its eyes tracking beyond Lorenna and the goblin male.

He slammed into her. Once, twice, thrice, and with a wicked grin, she could feel him quiver, the beast within the man skin quickened to blow his foul ejections into her most profound places.

He tilted his head back, a monster's ecstasy widening his jaws when, from the base of his throat, Lorenna saw shining steel sprout in a gout of black blood.

It was hot as it sprayed across her body, and inside herself she felt both cocks lurch in unison. The goblin's hands leapt to its throat, seizing the cold steel blade in its hands.

To her unending horror, Lorenna watched as the skin was flayed from the goblin's fingers, the blade twisting viciously before disappearing as quickly as it had come leaving only a dark hole that oozed thick ichor in its place.

The creature disengaged itself from Lorenna, its dual members wilting to flaccid appendages, and she saw the scarred stableman standing there. In his hands, he held a modest sword, one meant for the rough work of killing and nothing more. It was not a tool that had seen hours of careful polishing only to be stored in a case made of precious wood. It was a soldier's blade and the time spent upon it was passed in smoothing its edge to a razor capable of slicing wide goblin flesh.

The goblin male whirled from Lorenna and she could see its mouth working. In terrible understanding, she realized that it was trying to say something, but there was no sound, only viscous bubbles that rose and broke in the black hole at its throat.

The scarred man stood with a tireless posture, staring at the goblin before him. Lorenna could see him looking intently into its eyes, searching, perhaps waiting. But it was not the goblin male that the stableman watched, it was the reflection in its eyes of the female who gathered herself for the attack.

She leapt, like a great forest cat, and long claws burst through the gentle hands of a noblewoman. Her snarl was cut cleanly in two as the swordsman moved, seemingly without effort, his eyes never leaving those of the goblin male. The sword flew with a vigor that would not have been believable had not Lorenna seen it with her own eyes. One instant and it was at the ready in the scarred man's steady hands, the next it flashed in a broad, shining arc, appearing to pass through the body of the female in mid leap as if the creature were made of only thin air.

Her mouth, stretched in the same horrid grin, twisted down into a small circle of surprise. Then, the top half of her body sloughed away along a diagonal line of her torso. The bottom half lost its balance as it landed just beside the scarred man, its feet slewing back and forth as it fell.

The goblin male came straight for the swordsman and then seemed to take him by surprise as it dropped to the floor, appearing to bow to him upon one knee.

Lorenna watched, her eyes wide and unbelieving, when suddenly the creature leapt up. In one of his hands, with the human skin fluttering like ribbons around the black-scaled claw within, it had seized the ankle of the other goblin. With inhuman strength, it flung the halved body at the swordsman, who was forced to jump out of its way.

The bottom half of the female goblin struck the wall behind the scarred man with a sickening thump, but already the other creature had the remaining half in its scaled hands. He held the torso by the long golden tresses of its head and began to whirl it around him in a two handed circle.

The swordsman regained his balance and with no hesitation walked steadily toward the beast as it whirled the half body by its hair around him. Lorenna could see that it meant to batter the man down as with an enormous bludgeon. As the circles began to take on speed, she saw the black and oozing body of the female goblin slip from within the skin of her mistress.

Too late, the male saw it for himself and the half body broke free to fall in a wet heap, harming nothing as it fell.

In its hands, the creature held only an empty human skin by the hair, and with a bubbling roar it stampeded toward the swordsman.

Lorenna could see his scar whiten, its jagged track running along his bunching jawline and down to disappear inside his shirt collar. She saw his knuckles tighten around his sword's hilt and everything seemed to happen in a long, drawn out progression.

The creature spread its arms wide as it burst forward, its claws springing free as it was about to slam into the stableman.

But as it approached, the scarred swordsman was no longer there, turning ever so slightly to the side and missing being raked by long claws by a hair's breadth.

Continuing his pirouette, as graceful as any dancer that ever lived, he came full circle as the beast's momentum carried it forward, and with a minor shifting of his grip, his sword whistled through the air to slice one of the goblin's arms off at the elbow.

The scarred man continued his flowing dance as he rounded the back of the beast and his sword lashed out once again with a flicker of movement that looked effortless. Only this time, when it struck there was the sound as if a bell had been rung. It was the sound of cold steel upon hard goblin bone and Lorenna felt tears welling in her eyes as the goblin's head toppled from its shoulders.

She had never seen anyone move like this man. She had never seen any *thing* move like him. It was as though she had witnessed the wind or the sea mastered by an indomitable will, something that should not have been possible.

He turned to her and she saw that he was unshaken, not even breathing heavily, and then the sword licked out, one last time, only now in her direction. Her numb arms tumbled down, her bonds cut cleanly, and she fell to the floor weeping. Blood ran freely from between her legs, but it was the sting of her tears that hurt the most.

They were bitter drops of relief and deliverance rolling down her cheeks, and she made no effort to hold them back.

She found him in the chateau's courtyard. His horse was saddled and he was dressed in the same manner as the day he had arrived. Of his sword there was no sign, although Lorenna did not doubt that it was near at hand.

Her throat was raw, her voice hoarse as she said, "I must thank you, sir. Whatever means are at my disposal, I would reward you for what you have done."

He said nothing as he adjusted the fit of his saddlebags. Silence had always been his way, she knew. What had just happened was of far less import to him than to her. This she knew as well.

"The danger is gone…for now," he said at last. "You owe me nothing."

"Nevertheless, I am in your debt, sir," she replied. "As it is, I do not even know your name."

He turned his back on her and bent down to the ground where two severed goblin tails writhed weakly, twisting and turning, knotting around one another.

"My name is not something I give lightly," he said over his shoulder as he tied the tails together with a length of rope and then mounted with them upon his horse.

"In any case, I leave you now and wish you well. It is time that I go back to another who once asked me my name. This time I mean to give it to her."

Lorenna said nothing more and watched as the grim man rode away, thinking of his vicious scar and his sword that rang like a sweet bell as he cut the monsters down. She knew that the secret of true names could become a precious thing if held long enough, and that to relinquish it to another was as much an act of love and faith as any gilded words.

She watched him until he faded into the distance, a dwindling shadow in the evening air. Then she turned back to the chateau where two bodies lay awaiting the bonfire they would raise this night.

The encamped army moved slowly, not yet fully awake with a spring mist lying heavily in the morning air

It had not been hard to find, even after all these months. The scarred man had only to inquire as he traveled. The faces of the voyagers he crossed on the way grew more and more hopeful, even if they were still fleeing away from the battlefront. The war had finally turned for the better, most accounts describing it now as a veritable rout. The goblins fell by the thousands with none to replace them.

He rode deep into blackened lands, the devastation of the monsters evident everywhere he looked. But he was reassured to find himself so far within goblin territory as he tried to rejoin the army. The beasts had been forced back and among the rotting corpses that lay strewn about, he saw only scaled, hideous beasts and nothing human.

And here, as he threaded his way forward and around cold campfires, he watched soldiers emerge from their tents rubbing at swollen faces and coughing while they poked halfheartedly among the extinguished coals. Soon, there would be pots of boiled coffee brewing and dark bread passed about.

He was directed to General Blanc's headquarters with a wave from one of his old compatriots. Except that there had been no smile of recognition, just a dismissive glance before pointing the way.

As he dismounted, there was movement from within the general's tent, and then the flap was pushed aside as the white haired man appeared, leaning heavily upon a pair of crutches.

His eyes grew large, then his mouth lifted with a smile that went straight to the scarred man's heart.

"Alexandre! Boy, I had nearly lost hope that I'd ever see you again," he said as he stumped forward.

Something or someone stirred within the tent, but then fell still in the moment following the general's words.

In the guise of a reply, the younger man turned to his saddlebags and after a moment's searching turned back to the general with a sack in hand.

He undid the cord tying it shut then dumped the contents out at the general's feet. Among a generous quantity of rock salt, two wrinkled goblins' tails were to be seen.

"Ah," said the general, "This is very good news, Alexandre...very good."

The general looked up at him with real gratitude in his eyes and said, "So few of you have returned. Far too few. But the tide has turned, although I can't say why, and the goblins can't retreat fast enough. Our bowmen spend half their time picking their arrows from the backs of fallen monsters, only to let fly again as they break before us."

The younger man nodded, then said, "Sir, I wonder if you could tell me where I might find General Grise? I have something for her."

General Blanc's smile wilted, with a grave tone he replied, "Sandrine? Sandrine Grise? Oh, Alexandre, I am sorry, but she passed through death's gate the day after you left."

"She had been at the spearhead of a tongs and hammer maneuver. Except that she and her immediate squadron moved in too fast. The rest of her men ended up mired down and too far behind.

Separated and alone, she went down fighting, but eventually the goblins picked her apart. The battle that day was won, but the skirmish was lost and Sandrine with it, I'm sorry to say."

The scarred man's eyes lost their intense focus upon the general before him. He appeared to scan the faces that moved through the shifting mist, searching for an anchor, searching for an alternative to what he had just heard.

"You know, Alexandre," the general continued, "When I assigned you to this mission, I mentioned that there were some doubts concerning you. I hope you understand that it wasn't from Sandrine. She had always been your staunchest supporter. When I discussed choosing you with her, she told me that you were a secretive man, but for all that, you were a man we could trust."

"There, on the ground at my feet, is the proof."

The younger man shifted his gaze back to the general, but it was without really looking at him, more like looking through him as if everything around him had become transparent and ghostly.

"But now that I have you before me, Alexandre, I have other news for you."

"The realm has need of men like you, men in which the kingdom can have perfect trust and confidence. The command has been issued for those persons who can devote themselves in perfect servitude to the law of the realm and to enforce it without question."

"You and the few others who have come back are to leave us once more, this time for good. Alexandre, you have been made Marechal. You will be the law and justice of the realm. You will be the unflinching servant of the kingdom."

The unfocused gaze, lost amid the general's revelations, tightened to take in what the white-haired man had said.

"You will ride for Barristide. It is not far from Urrune. Do you know of it?"

The scarred man visibly flinched at the mention of the second city, then said, "Yes, I know of Barristide. Good folk and good land."

"That's fine then, Alexandre," said the general, "You'll leave at once."

"Yes sir," the scarred man said, then continued, "And General, my name is not Alexandre. It never was. The records should show that Alexandre never left Sandrine's side and he fell with her in battle, for love of her and of duty."

The general dropped his gaze from the intense stare of the younger man, then looked back up at him, his eyes glistening.

He said, "Yes, Marechal. That is just what the records will show."

Without hesitation, the scarred man turned his back on the general and mounted his horse once more. His back was stiff with what the general hoped was purpose and resolve as he rode away, never once looking back.

From within the tent there was a quiet sound and then someone stepped outside to stand beside the crippled general.

"What we have wrought here today means our damnation, General Blanc."

"Yes," he replied, "I know. But I have been damned already and long ago, for so many reasons that I have lost count."

"He was the best of us. He didn't deserve this."

"No, of course he didn't," the old man replied, "But the realm deserves *him*. Together, you and I have birthed a man who shall be the perfect tool of justice."

"He has been wounded anew, annealed by a terrible blow to his courageous heart and because of that, he will never let anyone in, never lower his defenses or see his cold judgement impaired.

"It is what we both have planned. It is what was necessary. All that he had has been taken away, shorn from his life as a soldier, his love for another, and all that remains is his sense of duty."

"He will cling to that and make of it his identity."

The steel-haired woman stood still a moment, her lips trembling as the rider disappeared in the morning mist.

Then she whispered, "But at what cost?"

The old man upon his crutches knew that no reply was expected and offered none before turning away from the army and the grey-eyed woman at his command, to return alone to his tent, unaccompanied but for his conscience.

The End

The Chronicles continue with the story of Melisse and the Marechal in Volume IV, The Chase

Melisse and the Marechal de Barristide have survived a demonic battle only to find themselves at odds with one another.

A noble yet lonesome man, the Marechal would have her stay at his side while he searches for the evil behind hideous murders throughout the realm. Yet Melisse believes her destiny lies over the mountains, far from her past.

But that same past finds its way back to her and Melisse learns of yet another murder at House Perene. Only she is too late as she learns that the blood running in Helene Perene's veins is no more noble than her own.

Meanwhile, Silas has learned to play the game of intrigue and deception at the Estril court while he remains captive and consort to a High General's wife. Jealousy threatens his very existence but nothing will stop him as he strives for his own freedom.

Behind them all lies the broken tower of the Alchemist. It is a curse to anyone who falls under its shadow. In bitter chagrin, Melisse discovers she is no exception as she makes the attempt to unravel its terrifying mysteries.

An Excerpt from The Marechal Chronicles:
Volume IV, The Chase

"How long did you say he's been there?" said one man to another as they marched down a squalid alleyway.

"Rubio said at least three days, maybe four," the second man responded, almost out of breath.

The pace his companion set was fast.

"And you say he's been drinking this whole time..?" the first man said.

"Not me...Rubio," was the breathless reply, then, "Says he ain't moved in three days...just sits there, ordering bottle after bottle."

"Well, I have a hard time believing that," the first man said, "I mean I don't care who you are, a man's got to piss some time."

"I know. I don't believe it either. But Rubio says the fellow pisses only silver and his purse is a deep one. He says there might even be some yellow among the colors of his coin."

The first man stopped suddenly, then jabbed a finger into the other's chest. It sunk in a ways as the breathless man was more than a little fat.

"Nenouf, how in the hell did Rubio find this man in the first place? And before you answer, you know damned well I don't want to hear that *L'Anguille* and his slimy partner are involved."

His eyebrows bristled as he looked down at the shorter, portly man he had called Nenouf. Black as coal, his hair was almost blue and his regard just as dark.

"The Butcher's Boys don't work for that lot. Never have, never will…got it?"

Nenouf's lower lip trembled as he looked up at the other, then his eyes shifted down to the pair of meat cleavers hanging from his companion's belt.

They had been modified, their handles fitted with cross pieces just behind the wide blades and Nenouf had already seen on more than one occasion just how effective one was at blocking an opponent's weapon while the other crashed into living flesh and bone.

His eyes flitted back up to the man frowning down at him.

"Butcher…now, don't be mad Butcher, but it might be that Rubio got a message to go to that tavern, after all."

Nenouf had no problem admitting that he was afraid of Butcher. While he had never been a real butcher, the black-haired man's father had been. Right up until the day he had cuffed the son up the side of his head, as rumor had it. Seems that was when one of the very cleavers hanging upon his wide leather belt had found its way between the father's eyes in what was apparently a bizarre accident. As some said, a sort of occupational hazard, really.

"Ok," Butcher said and Nenouf could almost see steam starting to waft from his ears.

"Looks like I need to have a heart to heart with Rubio. Right after we get the job done," he said as he turned and started off again.

Nenouf hurried after him and heard him continue, "But not before we start counting all that silver and gold. Rubio is gonna have to come to terms with me first…"

Butcher whirled around and in his hand, Nenouf saw one of his long, thin knives. He knew that it had originally been used as a boning knife in his father's shop and that the thing was sharp enough to shave with.

"…because, if not, then…." and Butcher held the knife close to his own throat, then slid it slowly to the side.

Nenouf understood what the bigger man meant and was very thankful that he had not been the one to receive the message from *L'Anguille's* right hand man. For one thing, that man's reputation as a cold blooded killer was well known, even more so than Butcher's, and for the other, was the fact that Butcher could not stand the idea that anyone else was leading the way. Least of all being led by *L'Anguille* and his scary partner, Modest Klees.

The fat man caught up to the other, but not too closely, then they started off again down the dark alleyway where sewage lay piled up in building corners and where one could no longer tell the rest of the street from the gutters.

Dirty, all of it just so dirty, as was the thing they were about to do, Nenouf thought. A dirty deed, indeed.

Castang and Vinsou were waiting for them at the street corner opposite the tavern.

The two men were hulking figures, dressed as they were in great overcoats against the evening's chill.

Nenouf knew, too, that those overcoats served to hide the heavy weapons the two brothers preferred. Sometimes nothing more than a simple logger-man's maul, other times, veritable bludgeons fashioned to stove a man's head in with a single blow. Something at which both of the big men excelled.

"Butcher," one of them said. Nenouf could not be sure which. Neither of them moved their lips much when they spoke and their collars were upturned, hiding most of both their faces.

But a pair of dim blue eyes, the others, a dirty green, looked Nenouf up and down, then he heard one of them say, "Why bring little fatty?"

"Yeah," said the other, "No reason he gets a share of the pickin's, Butcher. Not when we's the ones what do the hard part."

"Shut yer traps, the both of you," Butcher said with a growl, "Rubio sent Nenouf to let me know, that's all. And, I'm the one who decides who gets a share."

A pair of muddy blue eyes narrowed at those words and the silence that followed was chilling.

One of these days, those three, are going to have at it. But surely not tonight, as there's bigger fish to fry, Nenouf thought.

"There's bigger fish to fry, right?" he said, cracking a smile and hoping that they would not decide to butt heads right then and there.

"What's fish got to do with it?"

Nenouf thought it might have been Vinsou who asked.

"Oh, that's just a finger of speech," the fat man replied matter-of-factly.

"What?" said Butcher, "No…it's a *figure* of speech, Nenouf. A figure."

"Are you sure, Butcher?" Nenouf asked, "I don't see what math's got to do with it. Besides I ain't never been too good with math…all that figuring just makes my head hurt.

"Now a *finger* of speech makes more sense, right. Like it points the way to what the person means to say. You see?"

The two brothers appeared to nod their heads slightly at the fat man's impeccable logic and Butcher grinned a brown-toothed smile.

"Yeah. Fine. Now let's go see what this fellow's about and maybe lend him a hand with his heavy purse."

He nodded in the direction of the tavern, then continued, "Lighten the load, if you get my meaning, boys."

"Oh, we get you, alright," said a muffled voice.

Nenouf still was not sure which one of the brothers had spoken.

They's like two peas in a pod, he thought, then smiled, thinking that particular phrase was a fine finger of speech, too.

Three men walked toward the tavern, their steps heavy and determined. Another man, rounder and shorter than the others, followed in their wake but not too closely, either.

Rubio shifted nervously on his stool. He had been sitting there for hours, waiting for Nenouf to get his message delivered to the rest of the Butcher's Boys. He took a measured sip from his bowl of beer, grimacing at the bitterness he forced himself to swallow.

The tavern owner frowned every time he made a pass with his broom in front of Rubio. The place was dead that evening. Not a soul other than Rubio and the drunken fool across the room from him. A third person was in the room next to them, of that Rubio was sure. Only that room was left in the dark, used only when the tavern was full enough to warrant lighting a fire in the second hearth and the rest of the oil lanterns that smoked with a sickly sweet scent of rendered fat burning.

He had heard the creaking of a chair from the shadows there followed just after by a faint snoring.

Doubtless another drunk left to sleep it off in a back corner.

It did not matter, in any case. All that mattered to Rubio was the man across the room from him.

The drunken man hung his head over a deep pewter cup, his hair unkempt and falling down to cover his face. From time to time, he roused himself just enough to lift the cup for a swallow or two, or when he found that he had emptied the thing and forgotten that he had, he would signal for another without bothering to look up.

The tavern owner kept as close an eye on him as Rubio, though, and whenever the fellow stirred, he was sure to bustle over with a pitcher of red and fill that pewter cup to the brim.

The wine that was poured was no local brew. Whoever he was, the man had coin enough that the barman poured him only a pale red wine brought hundreds of leagues from the north. Not the sort of vintage that any local folk would ever pay for themselves.

Rubio was amazed that the barman even had any on stock. Although, he imagined it posed no problem for him to send someone to buy up all that could be found in the other local taverns.

The man's coin gleamed bright silver from time to time and seemed to flow just as easily as the wine. That was the kind of coin that washed away problems like where to find good wine.

It was the kind of coin that men like Rubio followed, once he had been put on the scent with a message from the frightening Modest Klees.

None of the Butcher's Boys had ever seen Klees. They knew him by reputation only. And that reputation spoke volumes about the man that not one of them would ever want to meet, despite all their bravado.

Some folk called him *L'Anguille's Poignard,* the Eel's Dagger, and from the stories told of him, even if only a small fraction of them were based upon the truth, then he was not someone they would ever want to cross.

Butcher stayed away from *L'Anguille's* organization. Rubio could understand why. Their own little business got along well enough. A little blackmail here, some protection paid out there. Life and enterprise were relatively fruitful for all of them in the high mountain town of Haccia.

The community, itself, was the last outpost before the Ardoise mountains rose up in sheer spikes to form a natural barrier and frontier with the country that began upon their southern slopes.

In the region all roads, even the least cow path, ran to Haccia. In the high country, there was nowhere else to go.

Historically, people on religious pilgrimages had been part of the town's beginnings. For over a thousand years, they retraced the footsteps of a sainted man, looking for another reason to count themselves among the faithful and all that walking meant that when, at last, they had reached the village that gradually grew into a large town perched just below where the trees gave up and sheer goat paths among craggy rocks took over, that meant hungry bellies.

The residents of Haccia discovered how little effort it required to part these pilgrims from their last bit of coin in exchange for a place beside a warm fire and a bowl of hot stew.

Later, when swarthy men from the southern slopes discovered how to preserve their hogs flesh, commerce in the northern regions' mineral springs and the pink salt they found there anchored Haccia more firmly in place than any pilgrims ever could.

Salt and faith, it might have been the town's motto. Only it would not be a phrase concerning the religious zeal driving people over dangerous mountain paths to chase after the ghost of a man long dead. Rather, it would be faith in that the salt would never run out and that the southerners should never find another source so near.

Rubio's own father had been in the salt trade. The gambling and drink had done him in and the rest of the family with him. Their ancestral salt rights were lost in a game of dice, then his father lost himself headlong in a barrique of wine a few months later. They say drunks drown their sorrows. In his father's case, it was in the literal sense when he was found with his feet in the air and the rest of him facedown inside an upturned cask.

Creditors were merciless fiends.

L'Anguille and his Dagger were the worst of these.

The irony of the situation was not lost upon Rubio. Here he was preparing to waylay a drunken rich man and it was thanks to *L'Anguille* and Modest Klees that it was him, and soon the rest of the Butcher's Boys, and not some other rough folk about to make themselves rich. On the other hand, it was thanks to *L'Anguille* and his henchman that Rubio was seated there, a low scoundrel among scoundrels, instead of sitting before his own hearth, a comfortable home surrounding him and the family's flourishing salt trade business to keep him there.

Worse still, Modest Klees would take at least three quarters of whatever they found remaining in the man's purse. That was the part that ground Rubio most and would grind on Butcher even more.

Unless, they were to tell the Dagger that there was less than expected.

That was Rubio's plan. A simple one, but one that should calm Butcher down once the blood stopped running and the rich man a'kicking. Paying out a percentage would sting, but it would surely be for far less than whatever they really found.

The tavern keeper passed by him again, sweeping with his straw broom where not a speck of dirt remained, frowning as ever down at Rubio.

He did not care. He had paid for his seat with a cracked earthenware bowl of local beer. Hard to drink, as bitter as tree roots. But it would do to keep him there in his rights until the rest of the gang came to keep him company.

Rubio was sure it would not be long until they did. Then, in short order, they would have a drink of that pale red wine for themselves and something told him the coin that had paid for it would wash at least some of the bitterness away.

The pale red color shimmered just inches from the end of the drunken man's nose. He looked deeply inside his pewter cup and if he strained his eyes he could almost see her there in the bloody reflection of the wine.

He could remember how sweetly she had smiled when they had finally reached the summit and the southern passes that lay before them.

There were no trees at that altitude and even he had been out of breath, but mountain flowers ran through low grasses in every direction. The sight of them was like breathing air that no one else had ever breathed before. The purity of it invigorating.

He would have like to pick one for her, to see it tucked behind an ear, framed by her dark, flowing locks.

He would have liked to see her smile just once, if only once, for him and what he did for her.

Instead, she smiled at the valley running away from her to what she said was her future. And away from what she thought was her past.

"Melisse," he said, "It is not too late to turn back."

It was not the first time he had said those same words.

He had said them when she insisted they leave Licharre. Those same words lingered between them over the past two months as her desire to part grew more and more evident, until, at last, Melisse seemed unable to stand it any longer and the two of them headed south once more.

He had said the words again as they began the long trek up and up through foothills that grew ever more rude the further along they went.

And each time, her response had been the same. He did not know why he thought it might change now that they had passed over the worst of the mountains.

She turned to him and the smile upon her lips was fading away. Instead, he saw anger broiling upon her brow and in her deep brown eyes, red flame flickered.

He glanced down to see fine wisps of smoke rising from where her feet touched the ground. Her hands were clenched into tight fists and from time to time, a tendril of fire would slip from her grasp to coil in the air, as if hungry, searching for something to burn.

"Do you see this?" she hissed at him, "I can barely control it. You and your badgering about going back north to clear my name…it angers me that someone still tries to make my choices for me, Marechal.

"And you know what happens when I get angry."

He had given her his name and still she refused to call him by it. The scarred man stood there, forcing himself to not take a step back from her and the wild power slipping through her fingers.

"My name is Etienne," he said, "As you well know. I would not have told you if I did not wish you to call me by name. My real name."

His reproach appeared to penetrate the haze of defiance in her eyes.

Her brows came unfurrowed, then, slowly, she unclasped her hands and there was no flame, only the pink skin of a hale and beautiful woman.

"Yes, you did," she replied, her mouth softening from the hard lines of determination of just a moment earlier.

She turned away from him, as if to scan the valley far below, then said, "And you know why I don't call you that…Marechal. You try to bridge the gap between us with your own name. But I tell you once again that I won't close that distance."

The Marechal thought he saw her shudder, yet the wind was still.

"It isn't safe."

He heard some memory in those few words, something that weighed heavily upon the young woman's mind.

"As you say," he replied, "And as *I* have said, I would take that risk."

She stood straighter then, her back rigid.

"But you're wrong to do so. Whatever magic keeps you young and heals your wounds is no match for what burns inside me."

Then, lower, almost in a whisper, she said, "I can feel it, as I have before. It wants to burn you to the ground…"

He sighed at the resignation in her voice.

"The truth and your freedom lie in the direction of House Perene, not there where you believe accusations of murder will not follow you," he said.

"As it is, these strange murders of men skinned alive have followed you even here, Melisse. I do not believe that the demon we encountered in Licharre was destroyed, and, above all, whoever sent it certainly was not.

"Two months of calm have gone by, but do not be fooled. You are being hunted still and not by me. Further, these murders resemble too closely something I encountered a long time ago and there is no telling what might happen when the force behind them finally chooses to end the chase."

He did not continue on to say what he thought next. That the young woman before him was undoubtedly the prey.

"In any case, I cannot follow you. I have a task yet before me and where you say your path lies would only take me further away from it."

Still refusing to look at him, Melisse said, "What real good would come of my returning to the north? All the southern lands lie before me and I can lose myself in them and put myself far from whatever danger you believe looms in my shadow."

"Ah, but there is where you are mistaken, Melisse," he replied, "In their essential meaning, your problems are no different than any other's in that they will follow you wherever you go.

"Allow me to explain."

She made no sign that he should continue, nor did she that he should stop. Only her back remained just as rigid as her apparent determination to run away.

"My belief is that the encounter you had in the forest the night of young Perene's murder has somehow gone awry. It is possible, even quite likely, that the being who seduced you never intended that you survive.

"Otherwise, why allow you to see that it took the guise of the slops boy? A person you could easily recognize and who, doubtless, has since been found murdered and skinned like all the rest.

"And *that* reminds me of something from long ago. A time when monsters masqueraded in the skins of men. A base, yet effective, form of espionage. But those creatures were never so clever as to devise such a plan on their own.

"I think that something, someone, guided them in their efforts. Then, abruptly, it disappeared and took its knowledge with it, putting a sudden end to the slip skinned spies in our midst.

"Disappeared, that is, until now. For whatever reason, I believe it has emerged once again to mischief and as I swore so long ago, I will stop at nothing to destroy it."

Despite the flames that she held within her, Melisse's voice turned cold as ice.

"So, what you're saying is that this really isn't about me?" she said, "All your words that you could take care of me are only a pretext for keeping me where I am of use to you, Marechal.

"You desire that I stay not out of affection for me, but for your affection of the hunt. And I would be the bait."

"You misunderstand," he said, "When I was sent away to root out the goblins wearing men's skins, I had a lover I was forced to leave behind. She meant everything to me and by the time I returned from my mission, she was gone.

"In all my long years, it has ever been thus. I pass through time alone while those around me live out their lives then fall to dust. There have been women in my life, but never do they tarry at my side. Fate has always deprived me of that kind of happiness. Instead, I walk in solitude and remain faithful to the oath I swore when I learned of what happened to the last woman I ever truly loved and to whom I never had the opportunity to tell.

"I shall not rest until I find the one responsible, the one who forced me away from her side."

The Marechal's voice shook as he continued.

"I ask you to stay because I *do* care, and because I think the magic in your possession means that you could walk through time with me. That when my task is done, I would no longer see my future as a wasteland of solitude with no one to care for and no one who cares for me."

Melisse hung her head as she heard him speak.

"Marechal. You could be right. I don't know. Will I now live on as you do with the force that burns within me? It could be so. But you must understand, I am a bonfire only waiting for the spark to bring the blaze upon all who are near to me.

"Even," she took a step further away from him, "Even those who could matter to me. Very much."

He had not seen her face again as she walked resolutely forward to take up the trail that led down the far side of the mountain to foreign lands below.

And as always, it was to the back of a woman that the man said his silent farewell, before he, too, turned to return the way he had come. Only, as he walked his steps grew heavier, his back more hunched and he saw no more flowers nor anything else that might have been reason for smiling.

His side of the mountain was one of cold truths and hard rock, unforgiving, endless…and lonesome.

The wine glimmered in its pewter cup, tiny waves growing from its center that slipped to the edges to rebound and confound themselves, thus hiding the reason that there were any waves at all.

The man sighed and made no sign that he had heard anything as several men came through the tavern door to rejoin the one at the bar.

The wine shimmered and he simply wondered if its flavor would be less bitter for the salt.

Rubio heard the tavern door creak, then the dark figures of big men came looming into the tavern. The door nearly closed behind them, when a fourth man, small, rotund and as breathless as ever, slipped inside and said in a rush, "Rubio. I brought 'em like you wanted. Just like you said."

The barkeeper frowned and was about to open his mouth when Butcher cut him off.

"Best find a reason to go outside now. I think the back alley is probably a lot more interesting than it used to be. For the next few minutes, anyway."

The barkeeper's mouth hung open for a moment, then he closed it again, before mumbling something that sounded like, "Someone had better pay for the mess is all I'm sayin'."

Then he left without looking back.

Nenouf was still grinning in Rubio's general direction as Butcher leaned close to him, about to say something into the man's ear.

Before he could utter a word, one of the big men…it might have been Castang…said, "My Molly's got oxtail simmering at the hearth. I h'aint got time for any more discussin' when my belly's empty."

He shrugged his coat to one side and hefted what looked like a thick axe handle in his hands. It was missing the axe head, though. Instead, what appeared to be at least twenty heavy iron nails were driven through the business end, making of it a kind of crude morning star.

It made an odd whistling sound as he walked forward to swing it hard into the air where the rich man's head had been just an instant before. But rather than stove the drunken man's head in, it slammed into the table.

Nenouf watched, the smile still on his face fading as the scene played out. Castang, or maybe it was Vinsou, was pulling hard on his axe handle, but the spikes driven through it had been embedded fast in the heavy table top where the rich man had been sitting.

A man who was now lying on the floor with his own foolish grin on his face. Nenouf was sure it was only drunk's luck, but his head had lolled to one side just as the hard wood handle had slammed down, then overbalanced, the man had tumbled from his chair to the floor.

Butcher looked like he was about to shout something to Castang when Nenouf saw the drunken man roll over like a fish out of water. As he did it, Nenouf caught a flash of two things.

One was a terrible scar that ran down one side of the man's face in jagged lines like a bolt of lightning cast from boiled over skies. The other was the shine of bright metal in the rich man's hands.

It has only been for an instant, but it looked like he had meant to roll in the opposite direction. Instead of trying to get away, the fool had flopped forward, toward Castang instead, and brought the table down on top of himself.

The big man standing over him was still tugging on his weapon when the table started to fall, then Nenouf heard him yelp, then say, "Ow!"

It was like watching a logger man's tree begin to tip and fall. Castang...or Vinsou, it might have been...had flailed backward to avoid tumbling over the table collapsing before him. But as he did, he had let out a sound that was at odds with his size, the hurt sound of a little boy, as if he had been stung by a hornet.

For some reason, he could not stop his backward motion, then Castang was falling over and as he did, he reached toward his ankle with an anguished look on his face.

"Owwww! Garn! He done unhinged me foot," the big man shrieked.

His brother looked right, then left, unsure which way to turn. Butcher's eyes were narrowed at the improbable situation, but no orders were forthcoming.

Then, Vinsou was rushing toward his sibling lying on the floor, his own coat pulled to the side and a thick iron bar in both his hands.

Nenouf watched, his eyes wide, and as the second brother rushed forward, Nenouf shrank back behind the bar. He heard a terrible crash and popped his head up from behind the bar to see the second brother lying beside the first, his hand clapped to his throat and blood streaming through his fingers.

"Vinsou…Vinsou!" the first brother howled as he rolled from one side to the other, but even Nenouf could see the man was done for.

And over both the brothers stood that scarred man, staggering as he shifted his weight from one foot to the other. In one hand, he held what looked to Nenouf like a tiny, thin sword, not even a third as long as it should have been.

The drunken fool had somehow managed to put both brothers down, while he stood there close to falling over again. His free hand was at his belt, fumbling at a full sized sword still in its scabbard upon his hip.

Only his head kept tipping down and Nenouf saw that the man could barely keep his eyes open.

In a low, calm voice, Butcher said, "Rubio. Two paces to my left. We move in slow and steady."

Rubio nodded as he got up, his own battered blade sliding free from its sheath while Butcher settled his pair of heavy cleavers in his fists.

Nenouf knew that things were about to go to hell then and there.

But before they did, the drunken fool had something to say.

His voice was slurred and uneven, but he said, "She left me. After all that I did for her. After all that I would have done. She left."

His feet slid apart, then he narrowly caught himself from falling down again as he managed to place one foot wide before the other and turn himself to the side.

To Nenouf, it looked as if he wanted to address the wall off to the side of him and that, maybe, he had even forgotten the two men advancing upon him, slowly, yet surely.

He's going to get himself butchered good and proper like that, Nenouf thought. He don't even know enough to face those boys coming straight on.

Nenouf shook his head. The man might have had the coin to pay himself a pair of pretty blades, but standing sideways like that when two hard men were coming to take him down had only one likely outcome. And a drunk's luck only runs so far.

With an awkward jerk, the man managed at last to free his sword from the scabbard, coming within a hair's breadth of cracking himself on the jaw with its pommel as he did. Then, he tilted back before slumping forward, the sword's point driving into the inn's wooden floor as he leaned on it like an old man upon a cane.

"For my own good, she said," the man mumbled, his hair falling down over his eyes.

Rubio was grinning widely as he eased himself forward. Butcher kept his eyes narrowed, flicking his gaze from the scarred man's hands up to the face hidden largely by unkempt hair and shadow.

"Did you see that scar, Rubio?" Butcher said.

Nenouf watched as Rubio nodded, then replied, "He seen a battle or two, this one. Veteran, maybe."

Butcher nodded then said, "That's right. And he took out the tendon in Castang's heel, drunk as he is."

"So what do we do, Butch?" Rubio asked.

"We go in at the same time…exactly the same time," was the reply.

The drunken man's head hung lower still, then he mumbled, "She didn't wish to hurt me. But no one can. No one."

Rubio froze at these words, but with a scathing look from Butcher, he kept moving.

Then the two men burst forward, their weapons raised.

Nenouf shuddered, thinking he did not want to see what was about to happen, but he was frozen in place, fascination pinning him behind the bar, unable to look away.

Rubio's sword slashed in to strike first. Or, it should have.

But without looking up, the man's left arm raised the smaller sword up and with a slight flick of his wrist, sent Rubio's blade skittering to the side while Rubio followed it, his own momentum carrying him forward hard.

Butcher had rushed in at the same moment, but as Rubio struck out with his long blade to have it neatly deflected to one side, Butcher dropped down into a crouch, his cleavers slicing the air in sweeping curves that would take the drunken man's leading leg off at the knee.

The arc of those heavy blades meant for breaking bone and cleaving flesh was interrupted before they ever got there.

As Rubio's sword was slapped aside, he could not stop his forward motion, coming in close to the man who then took a sliding half step backward as he struck Rubio hard behind the ear with the butt of his *main-gauche*. Rubio's eyes were already rolling back in his head as he fell which was probably a mercy, because he fell hard just in front of Butcher and his cleavers.

The first one took Rubio in under the jaw and came crashing out from the tip of his chin in an explosion of bone and blood. The second landed dead center in the unfortunate man's forehead, sinking in deep.

Butcher let go of the cleaver buried in his business partner's brains while holding on to the other as he rolled to the side before springing up to his feet, a long boning knife already in his free hand.

Castang lowed like a lost cow from the floor while his brother lay still beside him, his hand having fallen away from the gash at his throat, the blood no longer flowing.

Butcher grinned his brown toothed smile and said, "Good enough. You helped narrow the split down to one man and that suits me just fine. Only I'm not like those three and you're drunk as hell."

The man opposite him did not seem to notice as Butcher edged further to one side, putting himself almost at the man's back.

Then Butcher burst forward, his boning knife weaving from right to left, while he held the cleaver high and ready to lop off a hand at the wrist if he could.

Nenouf did not notice that his own mouth was held in a perfect circle of surprise. Only one of the Butcher's Boys was still standing and it was Butcher himself.

It should not have been possible and what was worse was that they had been done in by a drunken man.

What kind of unholy terror might he be when he's sober, thought Nenouf, knowing full well that if he knew what was good for him, he should already be well on his way out the back door of the tavern.

But what he saw next kept him right where he was.

Butcher pounded forward just as the scarred man stumbled and pivoted at the same time. The sword that served him as a cane came with him, then it punched down again, only this time the point landed directly in Castang's thigh.

The big man lying on the floor screamed a high pitched scream and as he instinctively clapped his hands to the wound, Nenouf saw the ends of his fingers fly away at the same time the scarred man ripped the sword back up and into the air.

Blood squirted up in an arc from Castang's leg and Nenouf knew what that meant. A half inch to one side or the other and it would have been only a flesh wound. Instead, that drunken man had somehow punched through the artery in the big man's thigh and only red hot iron could save Castang then.

Butcher's boning knife whistled as it cut the air, its path about to carry it to land between two of the scarred man's ribs, probably to drive deep into his liver.

But, the man staggered back again, and Butcher's blade only tasted fine cotton fabric as it licked cleanly through the man's shirt.

Butcher kept going and spun round in a roundhouse circle, his cleaver cutting the air, but the scarred man had stumbled to one side as he raised his long bladed sword at last.

The cleaver struck it hard and Nenouf saw sparks flash as cold metal struck metal.

The heavy cleaver in Butcher's hand pulled him after it as it ran along the long sword blade. Nenouf saw his eyes go wide, then the short sword flickered in the scarred man's other hand.

Somehow he had twisted around, keeping his balance when he should have fallen. Instead, he had turned with all the fluidity of a dancer, his sidelong stance allowing him to move unhindered.

And in a shining flash, Nenouf saw the tip of that short blade pop out the far side of Butcher's neck, then disappear again just as quickly.

The drunken man stumbled back against a chair, then sat down heavily while Butcher staggered upright from being bent over only to fall back down again, letting go at last the cleaver and the boning knife. A few seconds later there was a strange drumming sound. It was one of Butcher's feet jittering on the floorboards then eventually it went as still as the rest of him.

Silence fell as the blood ran.

Silence remained when the blood stopped.

Then the scarred man said, "No one can…."

Nenouf shrunk down behind the bar, his arms hugging his sides tightly, barely daring to breathe. He was still trying to work out just what happened and how it had when he heard a faint sound from the darkened room next to the bar, there where no one should have been.

"*Au contraire, Monsieur*," said a voice from a darkened corner of the tavern.

"Say what you will, and I *am* forced to agree that your skill with a blade is astonishing, but you quite obviously *can* be hurt. The woman of whom you speak, you say she left you for fear of causing you injury.

"But, it is evident that in doing so, she has wounded you more gravely than any sword could."

The scarred man stood up when he heard that voice. He stood there, looking vacantly down at the floor, then swayed upon his feet before reaching out to steady himself upon a wooden beam running from the floor to the ceiling.

"She left me…after all that I did for her…."

The man who had come out of the shadows nodded, his face quite serious.

"Nevertheless, you have acquitted yourself admirably over these…" he nudged Rubio's inert body with the tip of his leather boot, "…these vermin.

"And for that, my employer would like to speak with you. I do believe he would like to procure your services."

Steel grey eyes lifted up from staring at the floor as the man fumbled an instant then, at last, managed to sheathe his sword in its scabbard.

"My services?"

"Yes, of course. You, dear sir, have talents that will interest him greatly. In the capacity of a dispatcher of problems, naturally."

The big man looked at the other, but it was more as if he looked through him, seeing other vistas and other faces. The sorts of faces that slipped ever away from him and into the distance as he stood still. Alone.

"Allow me to introduce myself. My name is Modest Klees, and my employer is none other than Cuixart Bleu, sometimes referred to by the locals with the unsavory epithet, *L'Anguille*.

"He is the kind of man who is always in need of those who specialize and, most importantly, excel in the fine art of wielding arms. I am such a one, as are you."

The grey eyed man made no sign, nor did he move, apparently waiting for something.

"He needs killers, sir. And what a killer you are…."

Modest Klees gestured toward the door and the two of them went out. But not before the big man stopped, turning around to throw a small handful of silver to the floor, and mumbled, "For the mess…."

Nenouf waited a long moment, but not so long as to let the innkeeper find the courage to come back inside now that the noise of fighting was over.

He followed after the two men leaving the bar, but none too close either, nor did his miss his chance at scooping up a few bits of silver on his way.

The two men were already across the street when Nenouf dared to poke his head outside the establishment's door, a thick fog having descended the way it often did in the mountain town.

And thanks to that fog, Nenouf would almost manage to convince himself later that what he had seen following after them was only a trick of fog and shadow, a contrivance of his overexcited mind.

He had been about to follow after them when through the fog he saw what he first took to be a very large dog, only it paused to look back at him and when it did, he saw not a canine's face but an enormous lizard's muzzle grinning back at him with a smile that fairly bristled in shining fangs. The beast turned away from him then slipped quickly into the mist, and Nenouf would have sworn he saw it go upon six legs, five of them dark brown or green like the rest of its body, while one seemed less robust and, stranger still, colored pink.

As if it was newer than the others.

In the weeks to come, at night when the sounds of the mountain town died down in the evening, and Nenouf lay in his own bed, his thoughts would turn back to that extraordinary night. And it was not with much thought given to the scarred man they had had the misfortune of crossing that evening. Nor was it spent in thinking of the way he had moved, of the awkward, clumsy manner of a terribly drunken man while he dealt out death on all sides as easily as he breathed.

No, what Nenouf thought of when he could not help himself, was the dog that was really some kind of enormous, smiling lizard thing, and he thought of that pink foot and the pale claws that hit the ground as it padded away from him on six legs. A pink leg newer than all the rest.

Nenouf would shudder when he thought of it and remind himself that it was only a trick of fog and shadow. A simple contrivance of an overexcited mind.

And try as he might, he could find no finger of speech that could describe how awful that pink leg had made him feel...

OTHER FICTION BY AIMÉLIE AAMES

Her Billionaire, Her Wolf—The Novel
A billionaire romance unlike any other—

She watches him every day.

For two months she has spent each lunch hour studying the enigmatic man in a restaurant always filled to overflowing; yet, for two months he is there each day in a booth all to himself.

Sara thinks she is safe as she drinks in every gorgeous detail reflected in the bar's back mirror. She asks herself who he could possibly be, convinced he would never notice her...convinced that no one ever does.

She could not have been more wrong.

Chance brings them together and animal lust is unleashed. But what she never could have imagined is far from being the strangest part of this tale. For there are shadowy figures holding the strings offstage and the manipulation of Sara Renardine has only just begun.

251

This is the entire collection of novellas previously published in the series, Her Billionaire, Her Wolf—A Paranormal BDSM Romance

The novel also contains an all new bonus story, **Into the Nightlands,** *featuring several principal characters from Her Billionaire, Her Wolf.*

An excerpt from **Her Billionaire, Her Wolf—The Novel (A Paranormal BDSM Romance):**

There was a sound and then the elevator doors slid open revealing the silhouette of a man, his gaze downturned as he flipped stapled pages in his hands.

Without looking up, he stepped into the dimmed room and Sara marched directly into his path.

What was I thinking?

All thoughts of gratitude were gone. That he had come to her rescue in the restaurant, that he would make arrangements for her job…a new, exquisite silk shirt….

None of it mattered any more as she stood in his way, burning with red rage.

"Who in the hell do you think you are?" she said, wishing she could have shouted the words loudly enough to shatter the windows.

Then, instead of raising her voice, her hand arced up in the shadows. It was slow, yet not, passing through the air as quick as an adder's strike, yet time had stilled in the near darkness and it was as though the air was as thick as syrup.

Rather than slapping him hard across the face, Sara felt her wrist entrapped in an iron fist.

And absurdly, she wondered what was written on the pages that drifted down to alight upon her feet while the shock of his viselike grip still vibrated down her arm.

The beautiful lanterns of his eyes locked on to her own as he said, "Do you not know? Do you really not know?"

His voice was calm, but his tone was glacial.

Careful...you're on thin ice.

"I have no idea who you are," she said, then bit back the rest of what she wanted to say as his eyes softened.

"Then look at me," he said, his voice as calm as ever, "Right now, look at me and tell me who you think I am. The truth. All of it."

Sara took a breath, then said, "You tell people what to do. You are so used to doing it, that you don't notice anymore."

He stepped closer to her and the hand holding her wrist did not let go.

"You're arrogant. You think you're entitled."

Another half step closer as he pulled her hand to his chest, forcing her palm against him. Forcing her to feel him.

There are cracks under your feet.

"You think you own people."

His other hand went to her shoulder and Sara could feel the strong beat of his heart under her palm.

"And, you are brave. You step in when you see someone in trouble."

Then he touched the side of her neck and Sara's breath came more deeply.

"You are a knight. You saved me...."

Pinned in the amber lights of his eyes, Sara knew that it was already too late, the uncertain footing she walked upon had turned to water as she felt herself drowning in his beautiful gaze.

He bent down to her, his lips soft against her own, searching for truths other than her words.

She pulled back from him, just enough to speak, her own lips brushing his as she said, "But, that doesn't give you the right."

His mouth captured hers once more. Warm and velvety. She felt the light rough of a day old beard rasp gently against her skin as she kissed him back.

"You don't own me," she said, breaking away only to sigh as his hands slid down her sides, then back up again as he cupped both breasts. Strong thumbs drifted across the nipples studding her blouse, swelling even more under his touch.

"I told you I would give you cause for regret. Now, I shall give you reason for pleasure."

His voice was delicious in her ears, like warm honey as he continued, "And I can promise you that it will not be the last time, not for one nor the other."

Hands that could have crushed the bones of her wrist to powder only seconds before roamed freely upon her body. Strong fingers undid delicate pearl buttons.

"Turn around…now."

Divine Fornication—The Complete Collection (An Erotic Story of Angels, Vampires and Werewolves)

Episode 1—Seduced by the Angel

Claire Sawyer's life is about to change in a way that she never could have imagined.

Blind since a terrible childhood accident, she dies for the second time in her relatively short life only to find herself in the arms of an angeli being.

Is he her guardian angel, or the monster responsible for the deaths of her parents so many years ago?

Claire will search for her answers as she is swept up into events involving the divine and their relation to the vampires and werewolves that she encounters in her incredible journey to discover the truth.

Episode 2—Taken by the Vampire

Claire awakens in a hospital room to find a man sitting quietly, waiting for her.

Except that he is no ordinary man, adorned as he is with dark wings and burning in black flames.

Is it the angel of death, come to take her away at last? Or is he the lord of all vampires, come to steal the prize from his adversary, the Messenger, the being who has healed Claire's blindness? Flying high above the city lights in his cold arms, Claire shall find herself brought to a lonely fortress where blood drinkers await her and werewolves roam the darkness, all of them waiting for the ravishment to come..

Episode 3—Claimed by the Wolf

From certain death at the hands of vampires, Claire Sawyer finds herself surrounded by hundreds of wolves.

Are they her saviors, or the culmination of the doom that follows her at every turn?

Cursed or no, Claire must fight for her survival, even if that means becoming one of them, wolves in heat with just one thing in mind.

Episode 4—Redeemed by the Conqueror

In the stunning conclusion to the four part series, Divine Fornication, Claire Sawyer finds herself caught between vampires, werewolves and angels. Three races of beings willing to battle for the one thing they value most—Claire's eternal soul.

Will Claire's guardian angel return at last, in her final moments? Or, will she be lost forever to eternal damnation?

An excerpt from **Divine Fornication—The Complete Collection:**

....Claire seized the opportunity and slowly crawled away. If she could manage to put some distance between her and the fighting wolves, she might stand a chance.

As she eased her way forward, practically crawling upon her belly through the high grasses, Claire saw the edge of the clearing not far away. She gathered her legs under her, readying herself to jump up and run for the cover of the trees when someone stepped directly into her path.

"Going somewhere, are we?" said a young man's voice and Claire looked up to see him grinning down at her.

He was a wolf, but younger than Clash and Braze, she surmised. He had not yet filled out his frame, appearing gangly and awkward due to his height and long muscles that had not yet taken on the heavy mass of the adult wolf shifters.

Claire froze, not daring to move a muscle. The young wolf was in near full human form as he lifted two fingers to his mouth. A shrill whistle sounded, to be quickly followed by two wolves loping to his sides.

They lifted up, their limbs stretching and smoothing into human form. One was dark skinned and scowling, the other blond and fair with a smile that stemmed from true humor and not the irony of the situation before them.

The darker of the two newcomers spoke first, and said, "Rend, you have to take her back. When the leaders finish…and you know they will soon…they'll come looking for her."

The other, the one for whom it seemed all a joke, chuckled and said, "Shard's right. Besides, she's not that special. In the city, we can get all kinds of human chicks. It's really no big deal."

The first wolf, the one the other two had named Rend, replied, "Yeah, but out here in the wild, human bitches don't happen every day. I might never get another chance."

Claire could feel her blood boiling as the young wolves spoke. as the young wolves spoke. She did not want to be simply an object to their adolescent desires, but she could not deny that the three young men standing above her were making her thighs part of their own volition.

"Now wait," she said, "You…you're from the city?"

The comic blond wolf nodded and said, "Yeah. My name's Flair. I came with Braze and the rest of our pack to help get you from the vampires."

"Ok," she said, "Just give me a second to think."

Claire desperately searched for a means of bargaining her way back to the city with the help of the young, blond wolf. Afterward, she was sure it would be far easier to escape from him than from the huge man called Braze.

"No," said Rend, "I've heard about you humans and how much you love to talk. I'm not interested.

"Shard, grab her arms."

The dark wolf never stopped scowling but he trapped Claire's wrists in his hands. He might not have been a fully grown wolf, but his strength was far greater than her own. She pulled desperately away from him, but his hold upon her did not ease.

"Flair, take a leg, already."

The blond simply shrugged as he latched on to one of Claire's ankles.

Rend eased himself then between Claire's thighs and she could feel him trembling as he knelt down to the ground, his own legs brushing against her.

Claire said, "You've never done this."

The wolf did not reply….

Anna, Collected and Corrected (A Paranormal BDSM Story Collection)

An excerpt from Anna, Collected and Corrected (A Paranormal BDSM Story), a collection of the series, **Anna Ixstassou, A Reluctant Witch in the Land of BDSM:**

He pulls the cord that runs from my wrists up through a pulley above my head. My arms rise higher and I feel the low ache in my shoulders flame up in protest. I'm on the tips of my toes now, my calves are starting to burn and I can't help it if every time he makes an adjustment I only get wetter.

I should've known better, being who I am. Or, maybe, that's the reason why I didn't see this coming. Too close, too blind to remark what should have been obvious from the start.

The pulley creaks with my weight and a quiet whimper escapes through my lips. I bite down any other sound that might try to get by my guard. The master is exigent and will only make me pay if I don't follow his rules to the letter.

He doesn't notice, though, as he ties off the thin rope at a little T post thing. It reminds me of something I once saw on a sailboat, only smaller, and that seems just about right for this guy. A sailboat type...no, a yacht type of guy. He has it written all over him, with his broad chest and heavy arms. I've never seen anyone with shoulders so square. It's as if he was press formed in a mold destined to turn out lovely men. Which is what he is. Lovely, gorgeous, take your pick of whatever man candy euphemism strikes your fancy. He's all that and then some.

He bends down now and slides his hand down across my bare belly. It's flat and tight. I bust my ass at the gym and skip the pasta. The price to pay for abs that make men want to touch me, to lick me up and down like a lollipop.

He keeps going down with his hand and slips it in between my thighs, pausing just for a moment at my aching, wet epicenter. He knows I'm turned on, but refuses me and my needs, sliding his hand down my legs instead. At my ankles are a pair of leather straps that he buckles around each, cinching them in tight before finally descending to the tiny platform where I'm standing. I didn't notice before but it's actually two platforms that he unlatches and pushes apart. They follow the track of the half circle rail mounted to the wall behind me. The effect is that suddenly my legs are spread wide open and there's nothing I can do about it.

Do I care that much? It's hard to say. On one hand, what I went through yesterday with him at the controls was awful. He made me feel like absolute shit. On the other hand, I came back today, didn't I? Yeah, I did.

I think it's because he's just that beautiful. And, I use that word, beautiful, for a reason, because it isn't often that it applies well to men. Men are handsome, or rugged, or built. But this guy…he has it all. He owns the company I work for, he's built like the wet dream of a Greek goddess, and, right now, at this very moment, I'm what he's thinking about. I'm at the center of his every intention and filling his lovely green eyes with lust. And all of that's just fine except for one thing.

He's the devil.

There he is before me, perfect in so many ways…but the devil, just the same. You don't think you're ever going to meet the devil, right? That it takes a dark circle of naked worshippers off on some hill in the woods. It has to be at night, the moon up high and full, and the wind whispering of foul portents. There should be some blood letting first, then everyone whips themselves into a frenzied orgy that is meant to call up the dark one.

Only the devil takes so many forms. I know this. I am my mother's daughter, after all. But the only thing I had to do was to ask for a meeting with the boss. Mistake? You tell me once I get done with this story….

***

We took the elevator down and I had trouble not fidgeting or tugging at the mask I was wearing. Ewan was dressed in a full split tail tuxedo, with elaborate cummerbund and a golden pocket watch that he said dated to the twenties. It didn't matter to me as he was as resplendent as ever, his gorgeous hands housed within impeccably white gloves. He even wore a silk top hat which set his attire off perfectly.

He leaned upon a black cane, a roaring lion's head in ivory as its pommel, and looked me up and down.

After my bath, I had found my clothing, or what little there was of it, laid out upon the suite's bed. I was dressed in a body suit of black mesh that hid next to nothing of my skin beneath. A silver mask hid my face from scrutiny and I carried a sort of short whip that Ewan had called a scourge. It was comprised of many strands of soft velvet cording, like an overlong tassel, finishing in a black, leather bound handle that felt good within my hand.

I doubted that it could ever inflict real damage as soft as the strands were, but the heft and weight of it gave me the illusion that I could yet control what was about to happen.

In very short order, that illusion was wiped away.

The elevator came to a stomach fluttering halt and its doors slid open upon a great hall filled with animals and other queer creatures milling about. The rustling of elaborate costumes and voices muffled behind all manner of masks came to a perfect silence in the instant after we stepped into the room.

There might have been one hundred of them, two hundred, even. I could not say, but they each and every one stopped in mid sentence and turned to face us.

My thoughts were a ruddy mix of pride and fear under their regard. Pride to be found at the side of Ewan Crest, my master, and for whom all before us then inclined their heads in an unmistakable gesture of respect. Fear because I knew that Ewan was an extravagant man and that if this masquerade was meant for his amusement and those assembled here, then I would soon find myself the center around which this hub of decadent beasts would turn.

We stepped down among them and they parted like the sea before us. The murmur of their voices surged up in excitement and the line opening before our steps led to what appeared to be some sort of bizarre table.

Our steps were slow, measured, and as we move closer to the wooden contraption in the center of the room, a wolf faced man leaned in and said, "Oh, Ewan...the boxing is going to be wonderful this year."

Ewan gave no answer other than a slight nod then seized my arm as we drew near to what I had thought was a table.

It was not flat as any table should be, but a series of opened wooden compartments. The wood was old, its veneer polished and shining. The surface had been inlaid with marquetry of the finest sort. French craftsmen had placed capering animals etched in precious woods, their colors contrasting with the rest of the piece. There were astronomical symbols, of a quality meriting a place among the most precious works of black magic.

I looked at it and with a feeling of lead settling into my stomach, I could see that it was lined in red velour and in that interior, the velour would hold the form of a four limbed being. A human being. Its parts were articulated with heavy, antique hinges where the joints of a person would be but its soft interior could leave no doubt. It was as much a prison as an iron maiden rusting and blood stained in an ancient chateau, only lacking the needled interior to terminate its macabre charm.

Once closed it would hold a person completely. The only openings that I could make out were at the juncture of where a pelvis would fit, both front and back. There were also cutouts at chest level. Two of them through which breasts might be drawn and punished.

I looked to Ewan, alarm flashing through me, but he did not notice, his gaze intense and staring at the articulated device.

"Master…I can't. Not this time," I said. My tone was low, meant just for him, but he was uninterested.

He called out, "Strong Man! To me."

And the crowd rippled as the mountainous form of the man made his way among them.

I had already encountered him in Ewan's office and he was dressed in the same manner as then. He was enormous in every sense of the word. His height only diminished by his width, and his body sheathed in black leather leaving only his snarled crotch exposed.

He grunted as strode up to us, then turning to me, he picked me up as if I were but a doll, a trifle in his hands, and set me down into the nest of red velour.

Its color was that of blood swallowing me up and I screamed. I had been laid upon my back and I burst upward, my hands gripping the sides of what now felt like a coffin.

"No! No, no, no…."

Heavy hands forced me back down and then wooden doors began closing down upon me, locking me into place as surely as if I had been buried.

The last one was the one covering my face and it was Ewan who lowered it into place. His look was grim as I implored him through the slitted eyeholes of my silver mask, but without sympathy, he closed the lid, shutting me off from the world.

I was in muffled silence. I could not move.

I think that I became stark raving mad for a time as panic slipped into the cracks of the box, wafting into my mind and sending me into blazing insanity as I convulsed in terror.

Rough hands found my breasts and I could feel them being pulled through holes. I screamed endlessly, sure that my throat was bleeding with the force of it. The horror of being enclosed with no means of escaping carried me down the fly blown alleys of insanity.

My legs were stretched wide apart until I though my hip bones would crack and burst through my overstretched skin and then I felt the beginning of what would soon become an endless procession of fingers, tongues, lips and cocks that prodded at me, nudging me, urging me to respond in kind....

About the Author

I live in a land where giants have walked. Here, water springs cold and sweet from rocks cloven by legends in their passing. Stone edifices mark the countryside, risen hundreds of years ago. Devils stalk the foothills and comely maids with webbed feet lie in wait along rough mountain passages. France is my home and imbues all that I write… come with me, for a short while, and we shall venture among the dark, twisting paths together.

Made in the USA
San Bernardino, CA
14 December 2014